Helen Leah Reed

Miss Theodora

A West End Story

Helen Leah Reed

Miss Theodora
A West End Story

ISBN/EAN: 9783744749473

Printed in Europe, USA, Canada, Australia, Japan

Cover: Foto ©Andreas Hilbeck / pixelio.de

More available books at **www.hansebooks.com**

Miss Theodora

A West End Story

BY

Helen Leah Reed

ARTI et VERITATI

BOSTON

RICHARD G. BADGER & CO.

1898

The frontispiece and chapter headings are from drawings by Florence Pearl England, the latter being after photographs.

I.

The tourist, with his day or two at a down town hotel, calls Boston a city of narrow streets and ancient graveyards; the dweller in one of the newer avenues is enthusiastic about the modern architecture and regular streets of the Back Bay region. Yet neither of these knows the real Boston, the old West End, with its quaint tree-lined streets sloping from the top of Beacon Hill toward the river.

Near the close of any bright afternoon, walk from the State House down the hill, pause half-way, and, glancing back, note the perfect Gothic arch formed by the trees that line both sides of Mount Vernon Street.   Admire those old houses which have taken on the rich, deep tones that age so kindly imparts to brick. Then look across the river to the sun just setting behind the Brookline hills,— and admit that even in a crowded city we may catch glimpses of the picturesque.

Half-way down one of the quiet, hilly West End streets is the house of Miss Theodora—no, I will not tell you her true name.   If I should, you would recognize it at once as that of a great New England jurist.   This jurist was descended from a long line of scholars, whose devotion to letters had not prevented their accumulating a fair amount of wealth.   Much of this wealth had fallen to the jurist, Miss Theodora's father, with whom at first everything went well, and then everything badly.

It was not entirely the great man's extravagance that wrought the mischief, although many stories were long told of his too liberal hospitality and lavish expenditure. He came, however, of a generous race; it was a cousin of his who divided a small fortune between Harvard College and the Provident Association, and for more than a century back the family name might be found on every list of contributions to a good cause.

Yet it was not extravagance, but blind faith in the financial wisdom of others, as well as an undue readiness to lend money to every man who wished to borrow from him, which brought to Miss Theodora's father the trouble that probably hastened him to his grave. When he died, it was found that he had lost all but a fraction of a former fortune. His widow survived him only a few years, and before her death the family had to leave their roomy mansion on the hill, with its pleasant garden, for a smaller house farther down the street.

Here Miss Theodora tried to make a pleasant home for John, her brother. He had just begun to practise law, and, with his talents, would undoubtedly do well, especially if he married as he should. Thus, with a woman's worldliness in things matrimonial, reasoned Miss Theodora, sometimes even going so far as to commend to John this girl or that among the family connections. But one day John put an end to all her innocent scheming by announcing his betrothal to the orphan daughter of a Plymouth minister, "a girl barely pretty, and certainly poor." It was only a half consolation to reflect that Dorothy had a pedigree going back to John Alden and Priscilla.

Ernest, John's boy, was just a month old when Sumter surrendered; yet John would go to the war, leaving Dorothy and the baby to the care of his sister. Eagerly the two women followed his regiment through each campaign, thank-

ful for the bright and cheerful letters he
sent them. They bore bravely that aw-
ful silence after Antietam, until at length
they knew that John would never come
home again.

It was simply of a broken heart that
Dorothy died, said every one, for little
Ernest was scarcely three years old when
he was left with no one to care for him
but Miss Theodora. How she saved
and scrimped to give him what he needed, I will not say; but gradually her
attire took on a quaintness that would
have been thought impossible for her
even to favor in the days of her girlhood,
when she had been a critic of dress. She
never bought a new gown now; every
cent beyond what was required for living
expenses must be saved for Ernest.

Before the boy knew his letters, Miss
Theodora was planning for his career at
Harvard. He should be graduated at
the head of his class. With such a
father, with such a grandfather, Ernest

certainly must be a great man.   The
family glory would be renewed in him.

Little by little Miss Theodora withdrew from the world.   She had not
cared for gayety in her younger days;
she hardly missed it now; yet she was
not neglected by her relatives and old
friends — even   the   most   fashionable
called on her once a year.   These distant
cousins and formal acquaintances had
little personal interest in Miss Theodora.
Their cards were left from respect to the
memory of the distinguished jurist
rather than from any desire to brighten
the life of his daughter.

If Miss Theodora's invitations grew
fewer and fewer, she herself was to
blame, for she seldom accepted an invitation, even to luncheon, nor confided to
any one that pride forbade her to accept
hospitalities which circumstances prevented her returning.

II.

Although Miss Theodora disliked visiting, every summer she and Ernest spent a month at Nahant with her cousin, Sarah Somerset. She herself would have preferred the quiet independence of a New Hampshire country farm, but she thought it her duty to give Ernest this yearly opportunity of seeing his relatives in the intimacy possible only at their summer homes. This was before the days of Beverly's popularity, when almost every one at Nahant was cousin to every one else. Even the people at the boarding houses belonged to the little group held to have an almost inherent right to the rocky peninsula.

Both the little boy, therefore, and Miss Theodora were made much of by their kinsfolk; and the child thought these summer days the happiest of the year.

In other ways Miss Theodora was occasionally remembered by her relatives. Once she was asked to spend a whole year in Europe as chaperone to two or three girls, her distant cousins. Even if she could have made up her mind to leave Ernest, I doubt whether she would have accepted the invitation. She had almost determined never to go abroad again, preferring to hold sacred the journey that she and her parents and John had made two or three years before their troubles began.

For the most part, then, Miss Theodora repelled all attempts at intimacy made by her relatives. Unreasonable though she knew herself to be, she believed that she could never care so much for her cousins since they had all in such curious fashion—like swallows in winter —begun to migrate southward to the Back Bay. At first she felt as bitter as was possible for a person of her amiable disposition, when she saw people whom no necessity impelled leaving their spacious dwellings on the Hill for the more contracted houses on the flat land beyond the Public Garden.

Yet if Miss Theodora pitied her degenerate kin, how much more did they pity her! "Poor Theodora," some of them would say. "I don't see how she manages to get along at all. If she sold that house, with the interest of the money she and Ernest could board comfortably somewhere. Even as it is, she might let a room or two; but no—I suppose that would hardly do. Well, she must be dreadfully pinched."

Notwithstanding these well meant fears, Miss Theodora got along very well. The greatest sacrifice of pride that she had to make came when she found that she must send Ernest to a public school. Yet even this hardship might have been worse. "It isn't as if he were a girl, you know," she said half apologetically to Sarah Somerset. "Although he may make a few undesirable acquaintances, he will have nothing to do with them when he goes to Harvard." For Miss Theodora's plans for Ernest reached far into the future, even beyond his college days, and she must save all that was possible out of her meagre income.

Public or private school was all the same to Ernest; or perhaps his preference, if he had been asked to express it, would have been decidedly for the big brick schoolhouse, with its hosts of boys. What matter if many of these boys were rough and unkempt. Among them all he could always find some suitable companions. His refined nature chose the best; and if the best in this case did not mean rich boys or those of well-known names, it meant boys of a refinement not so very unlike that possessed by Ernest himself.

One day he came home from school later than usual, with his eye black and blue, and one of the pockets of his little jacket hanging ripped and torn.

"Why, what is the matter, Ernest?" cried his aunt; "have you been fighting?"

"Well, not exactly fighting, but kind of fighting," he replied, and "kind of fighting" became one of the joking phrases between aunt and nephew whenever the latter professed uncertainty as to his attitude on any particular question.

"You see, it was this way," and he began to explain the black eye and the torn pocket.

"There were two big mickies—Irish you know—bothering two little niggers —oh, excuse me! black boys—at the corner of our school; so I just pitched in and gave it to them right and left. But they were bigger than me, and maybe I'd have got whipped if it hadn't been for Ben Bruce. He just ran down the school steps like a streak of lightning, and you should have seen those bullies slink away. They muttered something about doing Ben up some other day; but I guess they'll never dare touch him."

Now, Ben Bruce, two or three classes ahead of Ernest in school, was a hero in the eyes of the younger boy. Ben was famous as an athlete, and Ernest, in schoolboy fashion, could never have hoped for an intimacy with one so greatly his superior in years and strength had not this chance encounter thrown them together. Ben appreciated the younger boy's manliness, and the two walked together down the hill, as a rearguard to the little negroes. The latter, too much amazed at the whole encounter even to speak, soon ran down a side street to their homes, and Ben and Ernest, if they did not say a great deal to each other at that time, felt that a real friendship had begun between them.

Miss Theodora heard Ernest's account of the affair with mixed feelings. She was glad that her boy had shown himself true to the principles of an Abolition family; yet she wished that circumstances had made a contact with rough boys impossible for him. She was not altogether certain that she approved the intimacy with Ben, whose family belonged to an outside circle of West Enders with which she had hardly come into contact herself.

An expression of her misgivings drew forth a remonstrance from Miss Chatterwits: "Why, you know Ben Bruce's father's grandfather was on General Washington's staff; they've got his sword and a painting in their front parlor." As Miss Chatterwits was an authority as to the biography of the meanest as well as the most important resident on the Hill, her approbation of the Bruces may have inclined Miss Theodora toward Ben. Yet, had he had no other recommendation, the boy's own good manners would have gone far to impress Miss Theodora in his favor.

Ernest never knew just how meagre his aunt's income was. He thought it chiefly lack of taste that led her to wear those queer, scant gowns. Year after year she drew upon an apparently inexhaustible store of changeable silks and queer plaided stuffs. Then she wore little tippets and small, flat hats, and in summer long black lace mitts, "like no-

body else wears," sighed poor little Ernest one day, as he asked his aunt why
she never bought anything new.

Yet even Miss Theodora's limited
purse might occasionally have afforded
her a new gown, had she not been well
content with what she already had. She
could not wish more, she reasoned, than
to have her old-fashioned garments re-
modeled from year to year by good Miss
Chatterwits.   .

Miss Chatterwits, who had sewed in
the family from the days of Miss Theodora's childhood, lived in one of those
curious short lanes off Revere street. It
was a great comfort to Miss Theodora to
have her come for a day's sewing with
her queer green workbag dangling from
her arm, with her funny little corkscrew
curls bobbing at every motion of her
funny little head. While she sewed,
Miss Chatterwits kept her nimble tongue
at work, lamenting the changes that had
come to the old West End. She knew

the region well, and understood the difference between the old residents and those newer people who were crowding in.

"It's shameful that the Somersets should think so little of themselves as to move from Chestnut to Beacon Street; and their new house isn't even opposite the Public Garden, but away up there beyond Berkeley Street. How aping the names of those Back Bay streets are, —Berkeley and Clarendon and Dartmouth,—as though American names wouldn't have done better than those English imitations! Well, Miss Theodora, we have Pinckney and Revere named after good American men, and Spruce and Cedar for good American trees. I wouldn't live on one of those new-fangled streets, not if they'd give it to me."

Then Miss Theodora, almost driven to apologize for her misguided relatives, little as she sympathized with them herself, would reply in words that she must have seen in some of the newspapers: "Well, I suppose the growth of the city's population makes it necessary for—"

"Fudge!" Miss Chatterwits would interrupt, "the West End seems to have room enough for lodging and boarding house keepers; and I guess it's big enough for true Boston folks. It just makes me furious to see "Rooms to Let," "Table Board, $3.50 per week," stuck up in every window on some streets. Goodness knows, I hope the Somersets like their neighbors out there on the Back Bay. I hear anybody with money enough can buy a house there." And a tear seemed ready to fall from her eyes.

III.

Ernest, himself, grew up without any social prejudices. His aunt often wondered at this, yet, like many sensible people, she did not try to impress him with her own views. As one by one the dwelling houses on Charles Street were changed into shops, he only rejoiced that Miss Theodora wouldn't have to send so far for her groceries and provisions. But Miss Theodora drew the line here. She had always been able to go to the market every day, and no thrifty housewife needs a provision shop under her very nose, she said.

Her one exception in favor of neighborhood shopping was made for the little thread and needle shop on the corner below her house. Even a person who doesn't have many new gowns occasionally needs tapes and needles, and may find it convenient to buy them near at hand.

This shop was a delight to Ernest, and in the days when his chin hardly reached the level of the counter, he loved to stand and gaze at the rows of jars filled with variegated sticks of candy, jaw-breakers and pickled limes; for the two maiden ladies who kept the shop sold many things besides needles and thread. In the little glass show-case, in addition to mittens and scissors and an occasional beautiful fan, and heaps of gay marbles, was a pile of highly-colored story books, "The Tale of Goody Two Shoes" and others of that ilk, and mysterious looking sheets of paper, which needed only the manipulation of skilful scissors to change them into life-like paper dolls with elaborate wardrobes. Ernest, of course, took little interest in the paper dolls,—he bought chiefly marbles; but his cousin, Kate Digby, whenever she was permitted to spend a day at the West End, was a devoted patron of the little shop, and saved all her pennies to increase her household of dolls. Indeed, she confided to Ernest that when she grew up she was going to have a shop just like the one kept by the Misses Bascom. If Mrs. Stuart Digby had heard her say this, she would have wondered where in the world her daughter had acquired a taste for anything so ordinary as trade.

A block or two away from the thread and needle shop was a shop that Miss Theodora abhorred. Within they sold every kind of thing calculated to draw the stray pennies from the pockets of the school children who passed it daily. Its windows, with their display of gaudy and vulgar illustrated papers, gave her positive pain. A generation ago ladies had not acquired the habit of rushing into print with every matter of reform; otherwise Miss Theodora might have sent a letter to the newspaper, signed "Prudentia," or something of that kind, deploring the fact that a shop like this should be allowed to exist near a school, drawing pennies from the pockets of the school children, at the same time that it vitiated their artistic sense.

Ernest, as I have said, grew up without marked local or social prejudices. Many of his spare pennies went into the money drawer of the corner shop, and much of his spare time he spent with the workmen at the cabinet-makers' near by. For little workshops were beginning to appear in the neighborhood of lower Charles Street, and some of their proprietors had cut away the front of an old house, in order to build a window to display their wares.

Ernest loved to gaze in at the shining faucets in the plumber's window, and horrified his aunt by announcing one day that when he was a man he meant to be either a plumber or a cabinet-maker. Among them all he preferred the cabinet-maker's. Everything going on there interested him, and the workmen, glad to answer his questions, showed him ways of doing things which he put into practice at home.

For Miss Theodora had given Ernest a basement room to work in, stipulating only that he should not bring more than three boys at a time into the house to share his labors. His joy was unbounded one Christmas when his cousin, Richard Somerset, sent him a turning lathe. Almost the first use to which he put it was to make a footstool, with delicately tapering legs, for his aunt's birthday. He tied it up in brown paper himself, and wound a great string about it with many knots.

"Law!" said Diantha, who stood by as Miss Theodora slowly untied the bulky package, "what's them boys been up to now? I believe it's some mischief."

"Now, old Di, you're mean," cried Ernest, dancing around in excitement in the narrow hall-way outside the bedroom door.

But Miss Theodora, as she bent over the package, tugging at the strings, caught sight of some sprawling letters that resolved themselves into "A birth-day Present from your LOVEING nephew;" so, shaking her head at Diantha, she responded, loudly enough for Ernest to hear, and with no comment on the bad spelling, "Oh, no, it's a beautiful present from Ernest." And then Ernest ran in and undid the rest of the knots, and, setting the footstool triumphantly on its four legs on the floor, said: "Now, you'll always use it, won't you, Aunt Teddy?"

Of course Miss Theodora, as she kissed him, promised to use, and kept her promise, in spite of the fact that the little footstool—less comfortable than her well-worn carpet hassock—wasn't exactly steady on its feet. But although she so thoroughly appreciated Ernest's thoughtfulness, Miss Theodora did not regard the footstool with absolute pleasure. She was by no means sure that she approved of Ernest's skill in handicrafts. She wondered sometimes whether she ought to permit a probable lawyer to spend so much energy in work which could hardly go toward helping him in his profession. Yet, after all, she hadn't the heart to interfere with Ernest's mechanical tastes, when she saw that gratifying them gave him so much pleasure. She never forgot her fright one day on the Nahant boat, when Ernest, barely seven years old, was missing, and she found him only after a long search at the door of the engine room.

"You'd ought to be an engineer when you're grown up," she heard a gruff voice say, while Ernest meekly replied: "Well, I'd like to, but I've got to be a lawyer."

She did not scold Ernest as she took his hand to lead him up stairs, and she even lingered while he tried to put her in possession of all his own knowledge.

"This gentleman," he said apologetically, "has been explaining his engine to me," and the "gentleman," rubbing a light streak across his sooty face, turned to her with a sincere, "That there boy of yours has a big head, ma'am, for machinery, and, begging your pardon, if I was you I'd put him out to a machinist when he's a little bigger."

The plainness of Miss Theodora's dress may have placed her in this man's eye on the plane of those people who regularly sent their children to learn trades. Although in her mind she resented the suggestion, she listened attentively to Ernest as he tried, with glowing cheek and rapid tongue, to explain the various parts of the engine. If Miss Theodora never perhaps had more than a vague idea of the functions of piston and valve and the wonders of the governor, over which Ernest grew so eloquent, she was at least a sympathetic listener in this as in all other things that he cared for.

IV.

When it came to machinery, Ernest
found his aunt much more sympathetic
than his usual confidante, Kate Digby.
As years went on, the childish compan-
ionship between the children deepened
into friendship. They began to confide
to each other their dreams for the future.
Kate modelled herself somewhat on the

accounts handed down of a certain an-
cestress of hers whose portrait hung in
the stairway of her father's house.

The portrait was a copy of one thinly
painted and flat looking, done by an ob-
scure seventeenth century artist.   It
showed a very young girl dressed in
gray, with a white kerchief folded around
her slim neck, and with her thin little
wrists meekly crossed in front. Whether
her hair was abundant or not no one
could tell, for an old-womanish cap with
narrow ruffle so covered her head that
only a faint blonde aureole could be seen
beneath it. Colorless though this portrait seemed at first sight, longer study
brought out a depth in the clear gray
eye, a firmness in the small pink mouth,
which consorted well with the stories
told of this little Puritan's bravery.

One of the youngest of the children
entering Massachusetts Bay on Win-
throp's fleet, the little Mercy had been
the pet of a Puritan household.   Mar-

rying early, she had gone from her father's comfortable house in Boston to live in the country forty miles away, a region remote and almost on the borders of civilization in those days. Not mere rumor but veritable records have told the story of the fierce attack of the savages on that secluded dwelling, of the murder of husband and man servant, of the flight of the wife and little children, and of their final rescue at the very moment when the Indians had overtaken them,—a rescue, however, not accomplished until one of the children had been killed by an arrow, while the mother pierced through the arm, was forced to drop the gun with which she held off her assailants.

"Just think of her being so brave and shooting like that!" Kate would say to Ernest. "I admire her more than any of my great-great-great-grandmothers — whichever of the 'greats' she was. And then she brought up all her children so beautifully, with almost nothing to live on, so that every one of them became somebody. I'm always delighted when people tell me I look like her."

"Well, you don't look like her," said Ernest, truthfully. "If you looked as flat and fady as that you wouldn't look like much. Besides, I don't like a woman's shooting and picking off the redskins the way she did. Of course," in response to Kate's look of surprise, "it was all right; she had to save herself and the children; but some way it don't seem the kind of thing for a woman to do! Now, I like her because she wouldn't let her oldest son go back to England and have a title. You see, her husband's father had cast him off for being a Puritan."

"Oh, yes, I know," responded Kate. "But I wish she had let him take the title. I'd like to be related to a lord."

Kate and Ernest were no longer little children when this particular conversation took place; but its substance had come up between them many a time before. Yet Ernest always held to the more democratic position; and as years went by his acquaintance with Ben Bruce intensified his democratic feeling. No one recognized more clearly than Miss Theodora this tendency of Ernest's, and she questioned long whether she was doing what John would have approved in sending him to a school where he must mingle with his social inferiors. In John's day public schools had been different.

An unguarded expression of these feelings of hers one evening at the Digbys' led to an offer from Stuart Digby to share his son's tutor with Ernest, that the two boys might prepare for Harvard together. Now, the idea of a tutor was almost as unpleasant to Miss Theodora as the thought of the undesirable acquaintances that Ernest might make at a public school. In the choice between unrepublican aristocracy and simple democracy she almost inclined to the latter; but Stuart Digby, her second cousin, had been John's bosom friend, and she could not bring herself to refuse the well-meant offer.   It was Ernest who rebelled.

"I don't want to go to college at all. I hate Latin; I won't waste time on Greek.   I detest that namby-pamby Ralph.   All he cares for is to walk down Beacon Street with the girls.   He don't know a force pump from a steam engine!"

But Miss Theodora, though tearful— for she hated to oppose him—was firm; and for three years the boy went down the Hill and across the Garden to recite his lessons with Ralph.   Out of school he saw as little as he could of Ralph. His time was spent chiefly with Ben Bruce.   Ben's father kept a small retail shop somewhere down near Court Street, and his family lived in a little house at the top of the hill,—a little house that never had been meant for any but people of limited means.

Yet from the roof of the house there was a view such as no one at the Back Bay ever dreamed of; for past the sloping streets near by one could gaze on the river bounded like a lake by marshy low lands and the high sea walls, which, with the distant hills, the nearer factory chimneys, even the gray walls of the neighboring County Jail, on a dark day or bright day, formed a beautiful scene.

There in that little room of Ben's Ernest often opened his heart to his friend more freely than to his aunt. Ben, considerably Ernest's senior, had entered the Institute of Technology—in boys' language, "Tech"—soon after Ernest himself had begun to study with Ralph's tutor, and Ernest frankly envied his friend's opportunity for studying science.

V.

In his boyish way Ernest enjoyed
life. The Somersets, the Digbys and
the rest made much of him, and at the
Friday evening dancing class he was a
favorite. Had he been a few years older
the mothers might have objected to his

popularity. A penniless boy attending the Friday evening dancing class is not old enough to be regarded as a danger-ous detrimental, and he may receive the adoration, expressive though silent, of half a dozen little maids in white frocks and pink sashes, without encountering rebuffs from their mammas when he steps up to ask them to dance. In this respect fifteen has a great advantage over twenty, emphasized, too, by the fact that fifteen has not yet learned his own deficiency, while twenty is apt to be all too conscious of it.

Children's parties had been within Er-nest's reach even before the doors of Papanti's opened to him. They were a friendly people on the Hill and no birth-day party was counted a success without the presence of Ernest. Simple enough these affairs were, the entertainment, round games like "Hunt the Button," and "Going to Jerusalem," and "Lon-don's Burning," the refreshment, a light supper of bread and butter and home-made cakes, with raspberry vinegar and lemonade as an extra treat.

· Miss Theodora herself did not take part in the social festivities of the neighborhood, although her silver spoons and even pieces of her best china were occasionally lent to add to the splendor of some one's tea table. Mrs. Fetchum was always anxious to make a good impression on the neighbors whom she sometimes asked to tea. Especially desirous was she to have her table glitter with silver and glass when Miss Chatterwits was one of her guests. Since Miss Chatterwits knew only too well Mrs. Fetchum's humble origin as the daughter of a petty West End shoe-seller, the latter could never, like the little seamstress, talk of bygone better days and loss of position. She could only aspire to get even with her by offering her occasionally a plethoric hospitality, in which a superabundance of food and a dazzling array of sil-

ver and china were the chief elements.
Miss Chatterwits had long suspected that
much of this silver was borrowed; but
she had never dared hint her suspicions
to Mrs. Fetchum, and the latter held up
her head with a pride that could not
have been surpassed had she been dow-
ered with a modern bride's stock of wedding presents. A day or two after a tea
party at which she had been unusually
condescending to Miss Chatterwits, she
ran across the street to return the borrowed spoons to Miss Theodora. It
was dusk as she entered the little door-
way, and she hastily thrust the package
into the hands of some one standing in
the narrow hall, Miss Theodora as she
thought, whispering loudly as she did
so: "Don't tell Miss Chatterwits I borrowed the spoons." For she knew that
the seamstress had been sewing for Miss
Theodora that day, and she wasn't quite
sure that the latter realized that the borrowing must be kept secret.

"It gave me quite a turn," she said as she told Mr. Fetchum about it. "It gave me quite a turn when I found that it was Miss Chatterwits; but I never let on I knew it was her, and I turned about as quick as I could. Only the next time I set foot out of this house I'll be sure I have my glasses."

It was hard to tell which of the two had the best of this chance encounter. Mrs. Fetchum consoled herself for the carelessness by reflecting on the presence of mind that had kept her from acknowledging her humiliation; and Miss Chatterwits gloated over the fact that she had caught Mrs. Fetchum in a peccadillo she had long suspected — borrowing Miss Theodora's silver.

In his early years Ernest had been a neighborly little fellow, and, alone or with his aunt, would lift his hat to a woman, old or young, easily winning for himself the name of "little gentleman." He wore out his shoes in astonishingly quick time playing hopscotch on the hilly sidewalks with the boys and girls who lived near, while Kate, to whom this sport was forbidden, sitting on the doorsteps, looked enviously on.   Willingly would she have exchanged her soft kid shoes for the coarse copper-toed boots of Tommy Fetchum, had it only been permitted her to hop across on one foot and kick the stone from one big square to another chalked out so invitingly on the uneven bricks.

But Mrs. Stuart Digby, although willing enough to let Kate visit Miss Theodora, made it a rule—and no one dared break a rule of hers—that Kate was never to play on the street with the children of the neighborhood.   Yet as she sat sadly in her corner, Kate, often referred to for her opinion on disputed points, at last came to have a forlorn pride in her position as umpire.

At length there came a time when Ernest's interests in the street games

waned. His former playmates saw little
of him. He neglected the boys and girls
with whom he had once played tag and
hopscotch, and some of the neighbors,
especially Mrs. Fetchum, said that he
was growing "stuck up." Miss Theodora hardly knew her neighbors by sight;
for it was one of the evidences of the de-
cadence of the region that the houses
changed tenants frequently, and furniture vans were often standing in front of
some of the houses near Miss Theodora's.

Mrs. Fetchum was a permanent neighbor. She had lived in the street longer
even than Miss Theodora. She always
called on new comers, and never failed
to impress on them a sense of the greatness of the jurist's daughter, with the result that Miss Theodora's comings and
goings were always a matter of general
neighborhood interest. Sometimes Miss
Theodora invited the children hanging
about her doorstep to come inside the

house, where she regaled them with gingerbread, or let them look through the folio of engravings in the library.

In spite of the lady's kindness they all stood in awe of her, as the daughter of a Great Man, whose orations were printed in their school readers beside those of Webster and Clay. Miss Theodora, with her quiet manner and high forehead, in a day when all other women wore more elaborate coiffures, seemed to the children like a person in a book, and their answers to her questions were always the merest monosyllables.

It was not worldliness altogether which took Ernest away from his former playmates. After his mornings with Ralph and their tutor, he had to study pretty hard in the afternoon. His evenings were generally devoted to Miss Theodora; either he read aloud while she sewed, or they played chess with that curious set of carved chessmen given her father by a grateful Salem client years before.

In little ways, Miss Theodora, though not a sharp observer, sometimes thought that she detected a growing worldliness in Ernest.

"Why don't we get some new carpets?" he asked one day.   It was the very spring before he entered college. "I never could tell, Aunt Teddy, what those flowers were meant to be.   When I was a little chap, I used to wonder whether they were bunches of roses or dahlias; but now you'd hardly know they were meant to be flowers at all."

This was true enough, for the carpet, with its huge pattern, designed for the drawing room of their old house, had been trodden upon by so many feet that now hardly the faint outline of its former roses remained.   The furniture, too, was growing shabby; the heavy green rep of the easy chairs had faded in spots, the gilded picture frames. were tarnished, and the window draperies, with their imposing lambrequins, were sadly out of fashion.   Yet from Miss Theodora's evasive reply the boy did not realize that poverty prevented her refurnishing the rooms in modern fashion.   He had everything he needed; but the circle of relatives all continued to say, "It's wonderful that Theodora manages as well as she does."

VI.

"Come along! Hurry up!" called Ernest to Ben, one winter's day, kicking his heels into the little hillocks of frozen snow on the sidewalk; and even as he spoke Ben, with a "Here I am," rushed from the house with his skates slung over his shoulder. Ernest carried in a green bag, on which his aunt had worked his initials in shaded brown, a pair of the famous "Climax" club skates, a present from his cousin, Richard Somerset. Reaching the Common, after a brisk run, they began to put on their skates.

The cold day had apparently kept many of the younger boys and girls away, and although there was room enough for all the skaters, not a few of them were objectionably rough and boisterous. Near the spot where Ernest and Ben were, among a small group of well-dressed lads, swinging stick or playing hockey, Ernest was sorry to recognize Ralph Digby.

"I wouldn't have come if I'd known Ralph would be here," he said regretfully to Ben.

"No matter, we needn't have anything to do with him," said Ben cheerfully. It was no secret to Ben that Ralph and Ernest, out of school hours, had little to do with each other.

"Well, I hate to go near Ralph," responded Ernest. "He always tries to make me feel small," and for the moment Ernest became uncomfortably conscious that the sleeves of his overcoat were a trifle too short, and that it had, on the whole, an outgrown look, for this was the second winter he had worn it.

"Don't take any notice of him, except to speak to him as you pass," said Ben.

"I know that's all I need do, but Ralph always seems to me to be saying to himself, 'Oh, you're nothing but a poor relation.' "

"Well, any way, he's a poorer skater," laughed Ben, and the two boys glided off, passing Ralph in his fur-trimmed coat, surrounded by half a dozen lads of his own kind.

It was this very superiority of Ernest's in skating, in his studies, in manners, that bred the ill-feeling in Ralph's heart towards him. Ralph was indolent in his studies and heavy on his feet. He looked on enviously as Ernest wheeled past him time and time again, and said to his friends that he didn't care to skate any longer. "There was too much riffraff on the pond." He was irritated, not only by Ernest's skill and grace in skating, but by the fact that his poorer cousin wore the famous "Climax" club skates. For a long time Ralph himself had been the only boy in his little set who possessed skates of this kind. They were a novelty and expensive, and the average .boy wore the old-fashioned strap skates. No one knew that he begrudged Ernest his glistening skates. Regardless of the sneering words wafted to them as they skated past Ralph and his friends, Ernest and Ben, with glowing cheeks and tingling blood, wheeled and curvetted until they were well-nigh breathless. At last, as the reddening western sky marked the end of the brief afternoon, Ernest, unfastening his skates, laid them on the stony margin of the pond, as he hastened to one of the Garden paths to help a little girl who had fallen down. _

"Where are my skates?" he shouted to Ben, who was still curvetting about.

"I haven't seen them. Where did you

leave them?" he called back, and in a moment was at Ernest's side. The green bag hung limp on Ernest's arm; he could hardly believe that the skates were not there.

"Well, at any rate we can ask about them," said Ben, and the two boys, Ernest somewhat forlornly, went about among the few skaters still left on the pond, asking if any one could help them find the skates. A few of the boys answered pleasantly that they knew nothing about them, the majority—and these the rougher—professed to be insulted at the question, adding, "I'll knock you down if you think I took your skates," and even Ralph was disagreeable in his reply.

"Perhaps some of your friends could tell you something about them; you always are chumming with such queer fellows—you never can expect much from canaille." Ralph always had a French word ready. As he spoke he looked at Ben in a way that made Ernest cry:

"For shame, Ralph !"

Ben's eye flashed. He lifted his arm, seized Ralph by the coat collar, shook him with some violence, and then turned on his heel without a word.

"That was right," said Ernest, approvingly. "I often wonder how you stand so much from Ralph. He tries to make himself so disagreeable."

"He doesn't have to try very hard," answered Ben; "he's disagreeable enough without trying," for Ralph never neglected to show that he thought Ben infinitely beneath him. A curt nod when they happened to meet was almost more irritating than a direct cut. Sorrowfully enough Ernest went homewards. His skating for the season, he knew, was over unless he should recover the skates. Generally, he did not look on the dark side of things, but this day he was disconsolate. In spite of Ben's assurance that the lost skates would be found, he was confident that they were gone forever.

Two days later Ben came to him with more excitement in his manner than was his wont.

"Would your aunt let you go over to the school with me this afternoon? I think we've spotted them."

Ernest rushed for his cap and mittens.

"Of course she would! She's out now, but I can go without asking." No explanation was needed to tell him that the "them" meant his missing skates.

"You see, I had my suspicions from the first moment," said Ben, "but I didn't dare say anything till I was sure. You know, there's one thing we never agree about, but I won't say anything until you hear for yourself."

Ernest was soon following Ben up the broad wooden stairs to the Principal's room. The master himself looked up with some interest as the boys came in.

"Yes, yes, I'll send for him at once," he said, after he had briefly welcomed them, "or, no, I'll take you to the room where he is," and before he realized where he was going Ernest found himself following Ben and the Principal into the large schoolroom, where fifty pairs of curious eyes were turned toward them.

"Brown, come here," called the master. An undersized boy, freckled, with small eyes near together, shuffled forward.

"Did you tell Jim Grey that you had found a pair of skates the day before yesterday?—answer—'yes' or 'no.'"

Not a word came from the boy, who held his head down sulkily.

"Answer—quickly—or home you go at once. Did you or did you not find a pair of skates?"

"No, I didn't," at last came from the reluctant lips.

"That's enough, sir!" thundered the Principal. "Now, Bruce, tell your story."

Then Ben, leaving the room for a moment, came back, accompanied by a man who carried a package under his arm.

"Yes, sir, that's the boy, sir," said the man with the package, pointing to Brown. "He came to my shop yesterday with these skates, sir," and he held up before the astonished eyes of Ernest his beloved skates. "He said as how they'd been given to him, and as he didn't have no time for skating, would I buy them, which I did, sir, for a dollar."

"A dollar," said Ernest to himself, pitying the boy who knew so little the value of a good thing as to let it go for next to nothing.

"What have you to say to this, Brown?"

"Yes, they were given to me," said the boy, doggedly.

"Who gave them to you?"

"A chap in a fur coat, I dunno his name. I was standing by the pond, and says I, 'Wot beauties,' when I see them laying there, and says he, 'Take them quick, they're mine, but I don't want to skate no more,' and he poked them over to me with his stick, and says he, 'Hurry off, or I may change my mind,' and they wouldn't fit me, sir, and so I sold them."

"A likely story," said the Principal. But two or three boys were found to corroborate this statement of Brown, one of whom was above suspicion as regarded truthfulness — the other two were somewhat doubtful.

"Are these your skates?" asked the Principal of Ernest, who, stepping up, showed his name engraved on the sides.

"Go to my room, Brown," said the Principal. "I will settle with you—and you, young gentleman," handing Ernest his property, "take better care of your possessions in the future." Then turning to Ben, "Thank you, Bruce, for looking into this matter. Brown has given me a great deal of trouble in many ways, and now I guess the best thing is to suspend him." For, although at the head of a Boston school, the Principal still clung to the colloquial "guess."

Ben and Ernest withdrew from the room under the fire of as many approving as disapproving eyes. There were, of course, not a few boys who sympathized with Brown, some from a class feeling, and others because they felt themselves to be kindred spirits of the culprit.

"How did you manage to find out about it at all, Ben? You're awfully clever," said Ernest, and then the elder boy explained that he had remembered seeing Brown just before Ernest left the ice talking earnestly with Ralph, and that when he came across the skates in a shop he made inquiries, which resulted in his suspecting collusion between the two. Though Ernest did not speak to him about it, Ralph felt that his cousin despised his meanness, and Ernest knew that Ralph disliked him all the more for his knowledge.

While his regard for Ralph constantly diminished, Ernest's fondness for Kate as constantly increased.

"She doesn't seem a bit like Ralph's sister," he would say confidentially to Ben; and Ben would echo a hearty "Indeed she doesn't."

Kate was never happier than when she had permission to spend the day with Miss Theodora. Paying little attention to the charges of Marie, her French maid, to "Walk quietly like a little lady," she would hop and skip along the Garden mall and up the hill to Miss Theodora's house. What joy, when Marie had been dismissed and sent home, to sit beside Miss Theodora and learn some fancy stitch in crochet, or perhaps go to the kitchen to help Diantha make cookies.

"Our cook won't even let me go down the back stairs, and I've only been in our kitchen once in my life; and I just love Diantha for giving me that dear little rolling-pin, and showing me how to make cookies."

Kate was almost as fond of Miss Chat-

terwits as of Diantha.   One of her chief
childish delights was the privilege sometimes accorded her of spending an afternoon in the little suite of rooms occupied
by the seamstress and her sisters.   Besides the old claw-foot bureau and high-
back chairs in her bedroom, the heavy
fur tippet and faded cashmere shawl—
either of which she donned (according to
the season) on especially great occasions
—Miss Chatterwits had a few treasures,
relics of a more opulent past.   These she
always showed to Kate and Ernest when
they visited her, as a reward for previous
good behavior.

Ernest was usually less interested in
these treasures than Kate.   He liked
better to talk to the green parrot that
blinked and swung in its narrow cage in
the room where lay the little seamstress's
bedridden sister.   But for Kate, the top
drawer of Miss Chatterwits' bureau con-
tained   infinite   wealth.   The   curious
Scotch pebble pin, the silver bracelets,

the long, thin gold chain, the old hair brooches, and, best of all, that curious spherical watch, without hands, without works, seemed to Kate more beautiful and valuable than all the jewelry in the velvet-lined receptacles of her mother's jewel casket. More attractive still was a shelf in the closet off Miss Chatterwits' bedroom. On this shelf was a row of pasteboard boxes, uniform in size, wherein were stored scraps of velvet, silk and ribbon, gingham, cloth and muslins —fragments, indeed, of all the dresses worn by Miss Chatterwits since her six-teenth year. As materials had not been bought by Miss Chatterwits since her father's death had left her penniless, a good thirty years before Kate knew her, the pieces in the boxes were genuine curiosities.

"Why didn't you ever get married, Miss Chatterwits?" asked Ernest one day when he and Kate were paying her a visit

"Oh, I don't know;" and the old lady simpered with the same self-consciousness that prompts the girl of eighteen to blush when pointed questions are put to her; and when Ernest, who always wanted a definite answer to every question, persisted, she added with a sigh, "Well, I suppose I was hard to suit." Then, as if in amplification of this reply, she began to sing to herself the words of an old-fashioned song, which the children had heard her sing before :—

When I was a girl of eighteen years old,
I was as handsome as handsome could be;
I was taught to expect wit, wisdom and gold,
And nothing else would do for me—for me.
And nothing else would do for me.

The first was a youth any girl might adore,
And as ardent as lovers should be;
But mamma having heard the young man was
      quite poor,
Why, he wouldn't do for me—for me,
Why, he wouldn't do for me.

None of the many verses describing the various lovers of the scornful young lady made so deep an impression on the children as the opening lines, in which she was said to be "as handsome as handsome could be;" and Ernest, who was a literal little fellow, said to Kate, when they were out of Miss Chatterwits' hearing:

"Now, do you think that homely people were ever handsome once upon a time?"

Now, Kate could never be made to call Miss Chatterwits homely. Indeed, one day, in a burst of gratitude, when the latter had lent the child her watch to wear for an hour or two, the little girl exclaimed:

"Oh, Miss Chatterwits, you are very handsome!"

"Nobody ever told me that before, Kate," said the old woman.

Then, with the frankness that in later years often caused her to nullify the good impression made by some pretty speech, the child added :

"I mean very handsome all but your face."

What could be a clearer case of "handsome is what handsome does."   .

VII.

Mrs. Stuart Digby scarcely approved Kate's fondness for Miss Theodora and her friends. Stuart Digby had married two or three years before John, and was living in Paris when the Civil War broke

out. His own impulse was to return at
once and fight; but as his wife would not
consent to this, they remained abroad
until Ralph was ten years old and Kate
four years younger.   Both children at
this time spoke French better than English, and Ralph for a long time disliked
everything American—like his mother,
who, not Boston born, professed little interest in things Bostonian. But in Kate
Stuart Digby saw the enthusiasm which
had marked his own youth, and he encouraged her in having ideals, only wish-
ing that he had been true to his own.

"Perhaps if I hadn't married so early,"
he would think—then, with a sigh, would
wonder if, left to himself, he might possibly have amounted to something. For
Stuart Digby was not nearly as self-satisfied as the chance observer supposed.

When he and John were at school he
had intended to study medicine, for his
scientific tastes were as decided as John's
bent for the law. But he had yielded all

too weakly to his love for the prettiest girl in his set, and an heiress, too. By the death of his father and mother he had already come into possession of his own large fortune. When these two independent and rich young people were married, therefore, a month after he was graduated from Harvard, it was hardly strange that Stuart put aside his medical course until he should have made the tour of Europe. Then, when once domiciled in their own hotel in Paris, what wonder that they let all thoughts of Boston disappear in the background? Just before the war what could the United States offer pleasure-seekers comparable with the delights of Paris under the Second Empire? They stayed in Europe until the beginning of the Franco-Prussian war, and managed to leave Paris just before the siege.

Not only the upsetting of things in France, but a crisis in Stuart Digby's business affairs, hastened him home at

last.   Besides, he felt a little remorse
about his children. He did not wish
them to grow up thorough Parisians;
already, young as they were, they began
to show symptoms of regarding France
as their country rather than America.
Disregarding, therefore, his wife's re-
monstrances, he broke up their Paris es-
tablishment, despatched his foreign furniture and bric-a-brac to Boston, and,
following soon afterward with his family,
bought a house in the new part of Beacon Street, a region which, when he went
to Europe, had been submerged in water.

Though some people fancied that
Stuart Digby could afford whatever he
wished, he himself thought otherwise.
After his return to Boston he found that
there had been a shrinkage both in his
own and his wife's income. There was
little danger that they or their children
should ever want, and yet the fact that
they had a few thousands a year less than
they had expected bred in them an un-

wonted spirit of economy. This spirit of economy showed itself chiefly in their dealings with other people. Stuart, for example, had always intended to settle a sum of money on Miss Theodora and Ernest, but now he decided to wait. He would help the boy somewhat in his education, and he would remember him in his will.

Faultless though he was in his address, elegant though he was in his personal appearance, Stuart Digby was by no means satisfied with the reflection that his mirror showed him. He had never expected at forty-five to find himself so portly, so rubicund. Idleness, easy living, and a steady, if moderate, indulgence in ruddy drinks will increase the girth and deepen the complexion of any man, no matter toward how lofty a goal the thoughts of his youth may have tended. In youth he had professed scorn for his own prospective wealth. He, as well as John, should carve out a career for

himself.   His money he would use in
certain philanthropic schemes. But falling in love had been fatal to this single-
mindedness,—and now, at forty-five,
what wonder that he was dissatisfied.

To saunter down Beacon Street to the
club, to play a game of whist with a trio
as idle as himself, to drive, never in those
days to ride, to sit near uncongenial people at a tedious, if fashionable, dinner, to
dance attendance on his wife or some
other woman in the brilliant crushes imposed on all who would be thought on intimate terms with society—this, he knew,
was not the life he had once planned. To
be sure, his footsteps sometimes carried
him beyond the club to a little down-
town office where he was supposed to
have business—business so slight that it
only irritated him to pretend to follow it.
To sign papers, to approve plans which
his lawyer and his agent had already
carefully thought out, this, he reasoned,
was almost beneath his notice; and so

after a time he gave up even going to the office, and papers were sent to his house instead for his signature.

He might, of course, have rid himself, at least partially, of his ennui, by engaging in some definite philanthropic schemes; but philanthropy as a profession by itself wasn't the vogue among rich men in Boston two decades ago. Even had it been the fashion, Stuart Digby could with difficulty have adjusted himself to the condition which this work imposed. His long residence abroad made it impossible for him to regard impartially his American fellow-citizens, whether looked at as an object of political or philanthropic interest.

Yet if Stuart Digby fell far short of his own ideal, there was at least one person in the world who believed him to be perfect; not his wife, not his son, but his daughter Kate, who was never so happy as when, clinging to his hand, she could coax him to take a long walk with her over the Mill-dam toward the Brookline boundary.

Moreover, it may be said without sarcasm that his many years' residence in Europe had made Stuart Digby of much more value to his friends in general than he himself perhaps realized. He had what might be called a refined and thorough geographical taste; this is to say, he was a connoisseur of places. He could tell intending travellers just what climate, what cuisine, even what company they would be likely to find at Nice, at Gastein, at Torquay, at certain seasons. He had many a picturesque and hitherto unheard of nook to recommend, and when the great capitals, especially Paris, were under discussion, he could pronounce discriminatingly upon the hotels and shops most worthy the patronage of a man of culture.

VIII.

"Yes, it was a pleasant funeral," said Miss Chatterwits, as she sat sewing one morning at Miss Theodora's. Kate, who was present, laughed at the speech, although she understood Miss Chatterwits' idiosyncracies in the matter of funerals. To the latter, funerals were sources of real delight, and few at the West End were ungraced by her presence. In her best gown of shining black silk, with its rows and rows of bias ruffles, she seemed as necessary to the proper conduct of the ceremony as the undertaker himself. With her wide acquaintance among the people of the neighborhood, she could decide exactly the proper place for each mourner; she knew just who belonged in the back and who in the front parlor, and the grave demeanor with which she assigned each one his seat hardly hid her air of bustling satisfaction.

Miss Theodora and Kate were therefore not shocked when she repeated, "Yes, it was a pleasant funeral," continuing: "I declare, I don't think there was a soul there I didn't know. I was able to be real useful showing them where to sit. You should have seen the flowers. It took us the best part of a day to fix them. The family, of course, felt too bad to take much notice of the flowers, but I guess they enjoyed the choir singing. Mary Timpkins herself would have been pleased to see how well everything went off, for she always was so fussy about things."

Then, as no one interrupted her, she continued: "It's just a shame, Miss

Theodora, that you did not go yourself. Mr. Blunt made the most edifying remarks you ever heard. Why, I almost cried, though you know I've had a great deal of experience in such occasions; and if you'd heard him I'm sure you'd have been miserable for the rest of the day."

Kate smiled at the thought of the pleasure her cousin had missed in escaping this misery, but Miss Theodora, not noticing Miss Chatterwits' humor, responded merely:

"Ah! the death of so young a person is always sad."

"Especially under such painful circumstances," added Miss Chatterwits.

"What circumstances?" asked Kate, now interested.

"Love!" answerd Miss Chatterwits, solemnly. "She died of love."

"Love!" echoed Kate. "Shakespeare says nobody ever died of love." Then, with an afterthought: "Perhaps he was thinking only of men. But why do you think Miss Timpkins died of love? She didn't look as foolish as that."

"Well,"—and Miss Chatterwits shook her head in joyful significance, for it always pleased her to have news of this kind to tell,—"I guess if Hiram Bradstreet hadn't gone and left her she'd be alive to-day."

"What nonsense!" said Kate.

"Oh, you can smile, but I've sewed at her house by the week running, and he'd come sometimes two afternoons together to ask her to go to walk somewhere; and even if she was in the middle of trying on she'd drop everything and run, looking as pleased as could be."

"Any one would look pleased to escape a trying on."

"Oh, you can make light of it. But once when I said I guessed I'd be fitting a wedding dress soon, she colored right up, and said she, 'Oh, we're only friends.'"

"That's nothing."

"Perhaps it was nothing when Mary Timpkins began to fade the very minute she heard Hiram Bradstreet was engaged to a girl he met on the steamer last summer. Why did he go to Europe anyway?"

"Probably because Mary Timpkins wouldn't marry him; for truly, Miss Chatterwits, I'm going to agree with Dr. Jones that she died of typhoid fever."

"Maybe,—after she'd run herself down worrying about Hiram Bradstreet."

"Oh, no. Hiram Bradstreet, worrying about her, fled to Europe in despair, and let his heart be caught in the rebound by that girl on the steamer."

This sensible conclusion, though at the time uttered half in fun, was characteristic of Kate. She was loath to believe that a well balanced girl could die of love. Love in the abstract troubled her as little as love in the concrete. She seldom indulged in sentimental thoughts, much less in sentimental conversation.

In their distaste for sentimentality, Ernest and Kate met on common ground; and even Mrs. Digby, though at one time disposed to discountenance their intimacy, at length decided there was no danger of her somewhat self-willed daughter's falling in love with her penniless cousin. In time, however, as Ernest boy-like, found his pleasure more and more in things outside the house, Miss Theodora and Kate drew nearer together.

The elder woman had always had a certain pleasure in acting as friend and helper to a little circle of poor people, of whom there were so many on the narrow streets descending toward the north. These were not the poor whites to whom Miss Theodora's mother had been a Lady Bountiful, but "darkies," as Diantha called them, of mysterious origin and of still more mysterious habits. They were crowded together in queer-smelling houses, in narrow lanes and alleys, or in the upper stories over shops in the squalid main thoroughfares of the district which some people still call "Nigger Hill."

"It doesn't seem a bit like Boston," Kate would say, clinging to Miss Theodora's arm while they went in and out of the rickety dwellings, where stout black women, with heads swathed in bandannas, or shoeless children in ragged clothes saluted them respectfully. Although Miss Theodora knew nothing of modern scientific charities, she tried to make reform and reward go hand in hand.

"I feel," she said occasionally, "as if I oughtn't to help Beverly Brown's family when I know the man is drinking; but I can't bear to see those children without shoes, or let Araminta suffer for food with that baby to care for."

"Of course you can't," Kate would answer, emphatically: "and Moses and Aaron Brown are the very cunningest twins any one could imagine, even if they are bow-legged." And then Kate, opening her little silk bag, would display within a collection of oranges, sticks of candy, and even painted wooden toys which she had bought on her way through Charles Street. "Come, Cousin Theodora," she would cry, "put on your hat and coat, and let us go down and see the twins, and let me carry this basket."

Or again: "There isn't any harm in my just getting some of this bright calico for aprons for Araminta, and you don't care if I buy mittens for the twins," she would say entreatingly; for Miss Theodora, always careful of money herself, often had to restrain her young cousin's expenditures, at least in the matter of clothes. As regarded food, it was different.

When Kate, stopping in front of one of the little provision shops, with their fly-specked windows, through which was dimly seen an array of wilted vegetables and doubtful-looking meats, decided to order a dinner for this one or that of her proteges, Miss Theodora had not the heart to hinder. But I will do her the credit to say that she never encouraged the giving of dinners to those whose need was caused by vice. In the future of the dark-skinned boys and girls Miss Theodora took ·a great interest. She realized that in the public schools they had their opportunity; and she saw with regret that not all who were educated made the best use of their education. Restless, unwilling to take the kind of work which alone was likely to fall to their lot, some of the young girls, educated or uneducated, drifted into ways which the older women of their race spoke of with the strongest disapprobation.

"They's a wuthless lot, the hull of them, and I wouldn't try to do nothing for them if I was you," Diantha often exclaimed, when Miss Theodora admitted how sorely the problem of these dusky people pressed upon her. Yet Diantha herself was almost certain to call her mistress' attention to the next case of need on which she herself stumbled in her wanderings among her people. Or, as likely as not, when Miss Theodora was sought out by some poor creature in real or pretended misery, the present emergency would overthrow all theories.

In one of the hill streets there was a home for colored old women, holding not a large number of inmates, but still holding, as Kate expressed it, "a very contented crowd" — much more contented, indeed, than many of the dwellers in the "Old Ladies' Home," the refuge for white women who had seen better days.

"I went to see old Mrs. Smith," said Kate one day, speaking of an inmate of the latter institution. "She was sitting with her blind drawn, looking as glum as could be. 'Why don't you raise the curtain?' I asked. 'You have such a beautiful view of the river.' 'Oh, yes,' she said, 'beautiful for anybody who likes rivers.' Do you know she'd rather sit moping in a corner all day than try to get some pleasure out of the lovely view across the river from her window! She enjoys being miserable now, just because she has seen 'better days.'"

"There are a great many people like her in the world," smiled Miss Theodora.

"Well, I prefer old Auntie Jane up in the colored women's home. She says that she never was as well off as she has been since she came to the home. She has a little window box with a small geranium and some white elysium in blossom; and she says that it reminds her of the old plantation where she grew up. She can see nothing from her window but houses across the narrow street; but she is a great deal happier than Mrs. Smith with all her view."

IX.

When Kate accompanied her on her round of visits, Miss Theodora did not penetrate far into the little lanes that zigzagged off from Phillips Street. She kept more to the main road, and seldom took the young girl upstairs, or down into the dingy basements. For in her mind's eye a large place was occupied by Mrs. Stuart Digby, who at any time might end Kate's visiting among the poor. Kate, therefore, had to content hersef with restricted vistas of fascinating

alleys with wooden houses sloping toward
each other at a curious angle, with little
balconies of strangely southern appearance; and she sighed that she could not
wander within them. She looked long-
ingly, too, at the little church whenever
they passed it; for Ben, who, rather for
entertainment than edification, went
there occasionally to the evening prayer
meetings, had repeated many amusing
speeches made by the colored brothers.

Still, if she could not do all that she
wished to, she made the most of what
came in her way. She loved to notice
the difference between the kinds of
things sold in Phillips Street shops and
in those of the more pretentious thoroughfare to the north, through which the
horse-cars ran to Cambridge. In the
former case, eatables of all kinds were
conspicuous,—not only meat and vegetables, and especially sausages, but corn
for popping and molasses candy and
spruce gum, all heterogeneously dis-

played in the small window of one little
shop. On Cambridge Street, oyster sa-
loons and bar-rooms and pawn-shops,
before which hung a great variety of old
garments on hooks, jostled against each
other, strangely contrasting with numerous cake-shops, which offered to the
passer-by a great variety of unwhole-
some comestibles. From the little windows of the dwelling rooms above the
shops, frowsy and unkempt women
looked down on the street below, and
Miss Theodora usually drew Kate quickly along, as occasionally they traversed
it for a short distance on their way to the
hospital.

In the same neighborhood was a short
street of unsavory reputation, partly on
account of a murder committed within
its limits many years before, and partly
because it held the city morgue. Hardly
realizing where she was, Miss Theodora
one day was picking her way along the
slippery sidewalk, with Kate closely fol-

lowing, when something dark crossed
their path. They stopped to make way
for it. It was a grim, indefinite something, which two men had lifted from a
wagon to carry into a neighboring building—a something whose resemblance to
a human body was not concealed by the
dark green cloth covering it. Then they
knew that they were near the morgue;
and while the elder woman was regretting that she had brought Kate with her,
she heard a voice speak her name, and,
turning, saw Ben Bruce but a few steps
behind.

"Isn't it late for you ladies to be in
this part of the city?" he exclaimed as
he overtook them, and they realized that
it was almost dusk.

"We are not timid," smiled Miss Theodora; "but we shall be glad of your
company, Ben. We stayed longer than
we meant to stay at the hospital, and I
know that I ought not to have kept Kate
so late."

"I wasn't thinking so much of the time as the place," said Ben. "Some way I do not like to have you and Miss Kate wandering about in these dirty streets—at least alone."

"I suppose you think that we would be better off with any slip of a boy. But truly we do not need a protector, although we shall be very glad of your company home."

"I do not mean safety exactly," answered Ben; "but it does not seem to me —well, appropriate for you and Miss Kate to go around into all kinds of dirty houses," and he glanced at Kate's pretty gown and fur-trimmed coat.

"Oh, it does not hurt my clothes at all," Kate answered, as he glanced at her dress. "I have only my oldest clothes on to-day, and I've been in a very clean place, too. I'm sure nothing could be cleaner than the hospital."

"Well, you can turn it into fun, but you know what I mean," said Ben. For like many another young man, he felt that tenderly bred women should be kept ignorant of the unsightly parts of a city. Thus as they went up the hill Ben and Kate kept up their merry banter, until they reached Miss Theodora's door.

"Come in to tea with us. Ernest will be glad to see you," said the elder woman. But Ben shook his head.

"Thank you very much, but they expect me home."

Nevertheless, he went inside for a little while, and sat before the open fire in the little sitting-room,—Miss Theodora allowed herself this one extravagance,— and heard Kate humorously relate the adventures of the afternoon.

"I have brought," she said, "a bottle of old Mrs. Slawson's bitters. I feel guilty in not having any of the many diseases they are warranted to cure, but I shall give the bottle to our cook, who is always complaining, and keeps a dozen bottles sitting on the kitchen mantelpiece.. You know about Mrs. Slawson, don't you, Ben?"

"Oh, she's the old person who made so much money out of a patent medicine."

"Yes, and then married a 'light-skinned darky,' as she called him, who ran away with it all. It is great fun to hear her tell of the large number of people she has cured. Why, the greatest ladies in Boston, she says, used to drive up in their carriages to patronize her."

"Why doesn't she keep up her business now?"

"Well, she is too old to continue it herself, and she does not wish any one else to have her formulas. She has just enough money to live on, and once in a while she has a few bottles put up to give away to her friends. My visits to her are purely social, not charitable, and this is my reward"—and Kate displayed a clumsy package in yellow wrappings.

Then Ernest came in—now a tall lad

looking younger than Kate, though a year older—and welcomed Ben, and begged him to spend the evening. But Ben, resolute, though reluctant to leave the pleasant group clustered around Miss Theodora's fire, hurried off just as the clock struck six.

X.

His father opened the door for him when he reached home,—his father in his shirt sleeves, encircled with an odor of tobacco. With an eye keener than usual, the boy noted particularly, as if seen for the first time, things to which he had been accustomed all his life—the well-worn oil-cloth on the hall, the kerosene lamp flaring dismally in its bracket. How different it all was from the refinement of Miss Theodora's home,—for although Miss Theodora's carpets were worn and even threadbare, and, except in the hall, she was as sparing of gas as Mr. Bruce himself, the odor of cooking never escaped from Diantha's domain. The indefinable between comfort and discomfort made the Bruce's economy very unlike that practised by Miss Theodora.

"You are late," said Mrs. Bruce querulously as Ben entered the dining-room.

"Am I? I met Miss Theodora and walked home with them."

"Yes, and went into the house with them, I dare say!" interrupted Mr. Bruce.

"Why not?" asked Ben.

"You always seem taken up with those people. I don't see how you can be, all so patronizing as they are."

"Patronizing!" repeated Ben to himself. "Miss Theodora patronizing!" How far from the truth this seemed!

"You do not mean Miss Theodora?"

"Why not Miss Theodora? She walks

along the street, never looking to the right or left, as if she were quite too good to speak to ordinary people."

"But she is terribly near-sighted. She does not see people unless they are right in front of her."

"I guess she could see well enough if she tried. I've noticed her cross the street almost on a run to speak to some little black boy. She's ready enough to take up with people like that; and she's able to see you. Ben,—but—"

Ben flushed a little. He did not like being put on a level with Miss Theodora's black proteges. Nor was this all. Mr. Bruce, taking up his wife's words, continued:

"Yes, it's just as your mother says; all those people think themselves a great way above the rest of us that are just as good as they are. I don't blame Miss Theodora so much, for her father really was a great man. But those Digbys! Who are they? Why, Mrs. Stuart

Digby's grandfather, they say, was a tailor in New York when my grandfather was one of General Washington's staff officers. We didn't have to buy that sword in our parlor second-hand in a Cornhill shop, where some people get their family relics."

"Not the Digbys or Miss Theodora."

"About the Digbys I'm not so sure. Miss Theodora ought to have some good things, if they didn't sell off everything when they went into that little house." As a matter of fact, the kin of Mr. Bruce were so few that Ben could not understand how he could generalize about them. Yet, "my family" could not have figured more largely in his conversation, had he been chieftain of a Scottish clan.

So rapid was Mr. Bruce's flow of language, that Ben and his mother usually kept quiet when he was well launched on any subject. Often, indeed, Ben let his thoughts wander far away until recalled to himself by some direct question.

It was Kate, Kate alone, whom his father's words touched. For the moment he felt that he might be perfectly happy could he see with the bodily eye as small a gulf between the Digby family and his own as his father presented to his mental vision. Seated before Miss Theodora's hospitable fire, watching the color deepen on Kate's sensitive cheeks as the light flickered across them, he forgot everything but her. In Ralph's presence, however, he realized that his world and the Digbys' were very far apart, and that his own awkwardness and roughness must be felt all too strongly by Kate. Then for weeks he would avoid Miss Theodora's house when Kate was there, or would run in for only a moment with Ernest to inspect some wonderful invention by the latter then in process of development in the basement workroom. Mr. and Mrs. Stuart Digby he seldom thought of. But how to bridge the gulf between himself and Kate!

The story of his own good ancestry began to have new interest for him. He looked more closely at his little sisters. They had the delicacy of feature which their mother still retained. They had the wax-like color which she had long ago lost. He glanced around the shabby room and felt rebellious. Should they be restricted to the same narrow life as their mother's? Was poverty to keep them down as it kept down so many of their neighbors? No, no! he would devote himself to building up a fortune, and then—even here Kate began to be curiously mixed up with his musings, and then he was called back to earth by his mother's voice.

The claim of his ancestors had never made a very strong impression on Ben. He had classed them with certain other harmless pretences of his mother's, like making a rug in the parlor cover an unmendable hole in the carpet, or putting lace curtains in the front windows of an upper room which in other respects was meagerly furnished. But now his point of view had begun to change, and he could even imagine himself in time bowing to the fetich of family.

"What's the matter, Polly?" he said one afternoon to his youngest sister, whom he found sitting on the doorstep by herself with the traces of tears on her face.

"Oh, Ada Green says that my new winter dress is only an old one because it's made out of an old one of mother's; and," incoherently, "she had ice-cream for dinner—and why can't we?"

"Who, mother?" laughed Ben.

"No, you know who I mean, Ada— they have ice-cream every Saturday, and she always comes out and tells me, and asks me what day we have ice-cream, and I have to say 'Never.'"

Ben, though he saw the ludicrous side of the little girl's grief, kissed her as he had many a time before when she had been disturbed by similar things.

"Cheer up," he said; "it won't be so very long before I can give you ice-cream every day, and new dresses not made out of mother's old ones. Then you can walk up and down the sidewalk and tell Ada Green; or you can offer her some of your ice-cream,—heap coals of ice on her head."

He added more of this nonsense until the child's face brightened as she entered the house, clinging to his arm, and mounted the attic stairs to sit near him while he studied.

Ben's plans for the future were definite, and his hopes were not the mere self-confidence of youth. Fortunate in securing one of the state scholarships at the Institute, he had been told by his teachers that a high place in his profession, that of civil engineer, might be his ultimately. But "ultimately" meant a long time yet, and his sister was perhaps right in sighing that before he could give her ice-cream, and similar delights, she would be too "grown up" to enjoy them.

When, therefore, he looked at his little sisters and thought of the probable narrowness of their lives unless he should interpose, he put aside any idle balancing of merits of his family as compared with that of Stuart Digby.

XI.

Ernest stood leaning against the mantelpiece in his aunt's bedroom. Never enthusiastic about college, he was growing even less so under the shadow of the impending examinations, now but a month away. His preliminaries had given him a hint that only by hard work could he enter college without conditions. Greek was the great stumbling-block, and he dreaded the final test more than he cared to admit.

"Do change your mind, Aunt Teddy," he began imploringly.

His aunt, in a low, straight-backed chair, looked up from her sewing.

"Change my mind about what?"

"Oh, you know—going to Harvard. Why must I go?"

Miss Theodora sighed. Had she waited and saved, pleased by the hope of a distinguished college career for Ernest, only to find college with him a question not of "will" but of "must"? Ernest caught her look of disappointment.

"Of course I am perfectly willing to go to Harvard to please you, but—I wish I could study the things Ben studies."

Miss Theodora's voice had an unwonted note of sternness in it.

"You are going to Harvard, Ernest, not because I wish it, but because your father wished it; because your father, your grandfather, your great-grandfather, five generations, all were graduates. You will be the sixth of our family in direct line to graduate with honor."

"Perhaps it won't be with honor in my

case, Aunt Teddy. Remember my Greek."

Miss Theodora smiled. "I have tried to forget it." Then as Ernest leaned down to kiss her, "No, no. I can't be coaxed into saying what I don't think. Of course you will go to Harvard and be an honor to your family."

He loved his aunt; he wished to please her; but, oh, if he could only beg off from college! If he could only follow Ben to his scientific school! Ben, no one could deny it, would be a great man, and Ben had not gone to Harvard. Ben and Ralph in contrast presented themselves to Ernest's mind as his aunt spoke of the "honor of the family." Changing his lounging position, he stood in an attitude of direct interrogation before Miss Theodora.

"Now, Aunt Teddy, which is going to be a great man, Ben or Ralph?"

"I am no prophet, Ernest."

"Oh, well, you know what I mean.

Would you rather have me grow up like Ben or like Ralph?"

"I am fond of Ben."

"Yes, and you don't like Ralph a bit better than I do. He can write Greek exercises that are nearly perfect,—and Ben don't know Alpha from Omega."

"You seem to believe that Ben's good qualities result from his ignorance of Greek, and Ralph's from his knowledge of the classics."

"I am not so silly as that, Aunt Teddy. But Ralph won't be a great honor to the family even if he should go through Harvard twenty times, and I wouldn't be a disgrace to you even if I didn't know Greek, or law, or any of those things."

As Ernest seldom spoke so bitterly on this subject, Miss Theodora wisely avoided further discussion by turning to her writing-table.

"I have a letter to finish now, Ernest; why do you not go down to your work-room? Kate is anxious for the table you promised her."

Ernest went off to his work, while Miss Theodora, still sitting before the fire thinking lovingly of the boy, pictured him in the not remote future a worthy wearer of the legal honor of the family. When Miss Theodora said "family," she thought most often of a long line of Massachusetts ancestors of dignified demeanor and studious expression, all resembling in general features the portrait of her grandfather hanging on the library wall. This portrait her own father had had enlarged from a poorly executed miniature. Perhaps it was the painter's fault that the nose had an air of intellectuality—even more exaggerated than that of the high forehead. Ernest as a little boy was so frightened by this portrait that he did not like to be left alone in the room with it.

As he grew older, it over-awed him like the rows of sheepskin-covered volumes in the bookcases under the painting. Miss Theodora, loving the books as she loved the portrait, occasionally would unlock the glass door with its faded red silk curtains to show Ernest the volumes that his grandfather and his great-great-grandfather had studied. As he grew older, she solemnly intrusted the key to his care, hoping that he would find the books as pleasant reading as she had found them in her girlhood. But the clumsy type and the old-fashioned style were so forbidding to the boy, that his aunt saw with sorrow that he made no effort to acquire a love for eighteenth-century literature. He managed, to be sure, to read the few "Spectator" and "Tatler" essays which she selected, and he discovered for himself the amusing qualities of Addison's "Rosamond." His "Robinson Crusoe" in modern dress counted of course as a book of to-day rather than as a work of the Age of Anne. Had it been among its sheep-skin covered contemporaries, more than half its charm would have vanished. The

Coke, the Blackstone, the Kent, which had been part of his grandfather's professional library, the boy regarded with even less interest than the other books. Miss Theodora had told Ernest that many would be as useful to him as they had been to his grandfather, not realizing that the mere thought of mastering their musty contents increased his distaste for the law.

Strangely enough, too, Ernest found little glamour in the name "Harvard." As a child he had been curious about the meaning of Class Day, when he heard caterers' carts rumbling through Charles Street on their way to Cambridge, or saw gayly dressed girls with deferential escorts walking toward the horse-cars or driving over the bridge. When he grew older the name of Harvard was associated with boat races and ball games, and it pleased him to think that he might some time count himself among the wearers of the victorious crimson. But the dreaded examinations and a truer knowledge of what the study of law meant had at last made the name of Harvard a bugbear.

While Miss Theodora, therefore, mused before the fire, Ernest in his basement workshop let his thoughts wander far afield from Harvard and the musty law. He wondered if he could make a dynamo according to the directions laid down in a new book of physics he had lately read. He wondered if he should ever have a chance to go West to the silver mines—for this was about the time when all eyes were turned toward the splendors of Leadville. He wondered if he should ever invent anything like that marvellous telephone of which the world was beginning to talk so much. He knew a fellow whose uncle had been present at a private exhibition of the new invention, and the uncle had been sure that in a short time people a mile apart would be able to exchange actual words over the wire.

As to the dynamo, Ernest felt pretty sure that he would make one; as to the mines of the West he was equally confident that he would see them some day; hadn't he always promised when he was a man to take his aunt on a long journey? But as to rivalling the inventor of the telephone, ah, no! what chance would he have to invent anything, when four years, four long years, must be spent at college, and at least two years more in preparing for the bar?

"Alas, Harvard!" sighed Ernest in the basement, while "fair Harvard" formed the burden of Miss Theodora's thoughts as she sat by the fire upstairs.

XII.

After all, Ernest entered Harvard
creditably. To work off two or three
conditions would be a very small matter,—so he thought optimistically at the
beginning of the year. On the whole,

college had an unexpected charm for
him, and he showed a temper in Novem-
ber quite different from that of the
spring. Perhaps the summer's tour in
Europe, which he had made with Ralph
and Ralph's tutor, had changed his point
of view. Miss Theodora could not feel
grateful enough to Stuart Digby for
sending Ernest to Europe. Though she
had herself set aside a little sum for this
purpose, she was only too glad to accept
her cousin's offer.

When the boys came home, their
friends noted a change in Ernest. Mrs.
Fetchum thought that it was largely in
the matter of clothes.

"You couldn't expect but what such
stylish clothes would make a difference,
at least in appearance; not but what
Ernest himself is just the same as he used
to be."

Justice drove Mrs. Fetchum to this
admission; for when Ernest, walking up
the hill a few days after his home com-

ing, caught sight of her as she stood
within her half-open door, not only had
he stopped to speak to her, but he had
run up the steps to shake hands; this, too
—for it was Sunday—in sight of several
neighbors who were passing, and under
the very eyes of certain inquisitive faces
looking from windows near by,—a most
gratifying   remembrance   to   Mrs.
Fetchum.

"Ernest looks some different," said
Mrs. Fetchum, describing the interview
to Mr. Fetchum, "but his heart's in the
right place.   He said he ain't seen a
place he liked better than Boston in all
the course of his travels."

Miss Chatterwits, who never agreed
with any opinion of her neighbors, de-
clared that Ernest was changed.

"But it isn't his clothes.   If I do make
dresses, I don't think that clothes is
everything.   It's his manners.   You can
see it, Miss Theodora,—just a little more
polish.   It's perfectly natural, you know,

since he's come in contact, so to speak, with foreign courts. Didn't he say that he saw the royal family riding in a procession in London, and didn't he and Ralph go to dinner at the American minister's at The Hague? Those things of course count."

Miss Chatterwits, like many others who take pride in their republicanism, dearly loved to hear about royalty. Ernest, therfore, when he found that she was somewhat disappointed that he could not tell her more about kings and queens, gave her elaborate accounts of the palaces he had visited. Thus did he half solace her for the fact that he had had no personal interviews with princes and other potentates.

Yet, although Miss Chatterwits would not ascribe any change in Ernest to his clothes, she by no means overlooked the extent and variety of the wardrobe which he had brought back with him from the other side. In this respect Stuart Digby had been as generous as in everything else connected with Ernest's foreign journey. His orders that Ernest should have an outfit of London clothes in no way inferior to Ralph's had been literally carried out. The result was startling, not only in the matter of coats, waistcoats and other necessities, but in the matter of walking sticks, umbrellas, and similar luxuries.

For almost a week Ernest kept the neighborhood astir counting his various new suits. Boy-like, he mischievously wore them one by one on successive days for the mere sake of giving Mrs. Fetchum and the others something to talk about. To Miss Chatterwits he gladly lent his cloth travelling cap, when she expressed her wish to take a pattern of it, and he let her carefully inspect a certain overcoat.

"It's quite at your service, Miss Chatterwits, although I more than half believe you are going to cut one just like

it for little Tommie Grigsby. Just think
of it, the latest London fashions for a
six-year old."

Nor did Miss Chatterwits deny the im-
plication. For in those days, when you
could not buy ready-made clothes in
every shop, the costume of many a little
West End boy was cut over from his
father's garments by the hands of the old
seamstress.

Miss Theodora did not find Ernest
changed. "Improved, perhaps, but not
changed by his summer abroad," she
said to herself, seeing in this no real contradiction. He was still the same Ernest
—respectful, kind, yielding to her will,
even in the many details connected with
the furnishing of his rooms at Cambridge
—the same Ernest who years ago had
clung to her hand dark evenings as they
walked home from Stuart Digby's. All
the interested relatives—"all," yet few—
wondered that Miss Theodora could afford to fit up Ernest's college rooms so

handsomely. But was it not for this that she had saved ever since John's death?

So Ernest, in Hollis, had the counterpart of John's old room; and his aunt, looking from the broad window-seat across the leafy quadrangle, unchanged in aspect through a quarter of a century, felt herself carried back to those early days. Until John's death she had not realized that all her hopes were centred in him. Now she knew only too well that life without Ernest would mean little enough to her.

Ernest, appreciating his aunt's devotion, tried to repay it by thorough work —tried, yet failed. For, after all, study is not the only absorbing interest at Cambridge. Sports in the field, practice on the river, these stir the blood and take a young man's time. A good-looking lad with a well-known name, connected with various families of reputed wealth and high position, has every chance for popularity at Harvard. But a popular man with limited means has to pay a price for popularity. Ernest spent his fairly liberal allowance to the last cent. He had to entertain, had to do things that were, though he knew it not, a great strain on his aunt's purse. Though he had entered college without the social advantages of a preparation at one of the private schools, he soon had many friends. Miss Theodora was pleased with her nephew's success. John had been popular, and it would have been strange indeed had the son not followed in the father's footsteps. She could not conceal from herself, however, a definite uneasiness that Ernest, unlike his father, showed little interest in his studies. He grumbled not a little at the course laid out for him, complained that he would have hardly a wider choice of studies in his sophomore year, and ascribed all his shortcomings in examinations to the fact that he was rigorously held down to uncongenial work. Nor was he altogether wrong, for many a Harvard student in those days longed for freedom from the fetters of prescribed studies.

XIII.

One Sunday afternoon in the early
May of his freshman year, after the service at Trinity, Ernest took his way toward the Digbys' house. Since midwinter
many things had tended to make him regard life less hopefully than before.
Just as his own shortcomings at college
were growing so evident that he could
not conceal them either from himself or
his aunt, the death of Stuart Digby cast
a cloud over him which made other

shadows dwindle. For he had been very fond of his cousin, and he sympathized to the full with Kate in her grief.

"Cut off in his prime!" said all the friends of Stuart Digby. "So much to live for!" "His life hardly half finished!" But, after all, death is as inscrutable a mystery as life itself. Stuart Digby had had his chance. He knew long before he died that his life, even if rounded out to the full three score and ten, could never be full and complete. He knew, as nobody else could, how far short he fell of the standard which he had once set for himself. He knew, with a knowledge that cut him to the quick, that, poor slave of habit that he had become, no length of life would place him again in the ranks of those whose faces ever look upward. He had had his chance. Why had he let it slip away from him? His life, so far as life means progress, was finished long before. He had not even accomplished the few definite tasks which he had set for himself. Among these was the making of some provision for Ernest. He had meant to give the boy a few thousands to smooth his path after graduating, or to leave him something by will. But death came so suddenly that this, like many other good intentions, was unfulfilled. Ernest, knowing nothing of these unfulfilled intentions, felt only a deep sense of personal loss in the death of his cousin.

A decorator had lately done over in the latest French style the room where Kate received Ernest. The high white wainscoting, the satiny sheen of the large-patterned yellow paper, the slender-legged gilded chairs, with here and there a lounging chair covered in pale green brocade, harmonized well with the sunshine that streamed in. Kate, in her black gown, seated at the old-fashioned inlaid desk in the bay window, but for her fair hair and glowing color, would have been the one discordant note in the

room.   The solemn man-servant had
hardly announced Ernest when Kate
rushed forward to meet him.

"Why, Ernest, I am delighted to see
you.   We were speaking of you today.
Mamma was saying that it seemed a long
time since you had been here.   She is
out now, and will be sorry to miss you."

"Well, it is longer than I meant to be;
but you know that I've really been very
busy, especially since the mid-year. I've
been trying to decide several difficult
questions."

"Oh, yes, I know.   How times have
changed, Ernest, since you used to play
hop-scotch with the Fetchum chidren,
while I sat, a mournful umpire, at Cousin
Theodora's door!   You used to say that
I was the best possible judge; and I
thought that you were always going to
let me help you decide difficult questions."

"It's just the same now, Kate.   I'd be
only too glad to have you help me out of
a good many things, if ——"

"If what?"

Now, however, Ernest dropped his serious tone. "If we were younger. Tell me, Kate, can you remember how you felt when you first realized that you weren't a child any more? I was thinking about myself the other day, and wondering why I feel so much older now than I did a year or two ago."

"Oh, it's going into college that is chiefly to answer for it. But I do think it's strange sometimes all in an instant we realize that we are older or different from what we were before. I really can't account for it."

"Yes,—I understand what you mean. You know those stone buildings that we pass on our way to the Nahant boat. Well, they used to seem to me mountain high, not only when I looked up at them, but when I thought about them. But one summer, years ago, I looked up and saw that they were not very high, nor very imposing. They were small buildings, compared with a good many up town; and then I felt that I must have changed."

Kate smiled. "Yes, I've been through just such things myself." And the conversation of the two cousins drifted on for a time, with reminiscences of the past.

"Ernest," at length said Kate somewhat abruptly to the young man, "after all you are more or less of a disappointment to me."

So far as appearances went, it was hard to see wherein Ernest fell short of the ideal of even so rigid a critic as Kate. Yet this well-formed, muscular youth, with his clear gray eye, seemed at this particular moment a little restless and uneasy as he fingered an ivory paperknife.

"How do I disappoint you, Kate?" he asked.

"Oh, in many ways. I used to think that you would be an inventor, or— something. But now—"

"I am nothing but a Harvard freshman," he broke in laughing.

"Yes, that is just it. You don't seem
to be ambitious; you aren't trying to
work off your entrance conditions; and
you didn't do well at the mid-years. You
spend very little time with Cousin Theodora. I'm sure I ought to feel compli-
mented that you've come here to-day."
As Ernest did not reply, she continued:
"Your aunt has always made such sacri-
fices for you that you ought to try to do
your best. Cousin Richard says—"

There she stopped.

"Well, what does Cousin Richard
say?" asked Ernest impatiently. But
Kate, remembering that Richard Somerset might object to being quoted, was
silent.

"Go to him yourself," she said at
length. "He will tell you." Then their
conversation passed to less personal
things, until it was time for Ernest to go.

Ernest, taking what Kate had said in

good part, pondered over it as he walked homeward. The afternoon was drawing to a close. Long afterward he recalled that walk among the flower-beds, glowing with tulips and hyacinths, with the last rays of the sun reflected from the little fountain, while the chimes from the church on the corner above rang out "Old Hundred." As he left the Garden and entered Charles Street all this cheerfulness was at an end. The houses cast shadows so heavy in the narrow street that he felt as if in another world. Somewhat depressed, he went up the hill to his aunt's house. From the parlor came the unwonted sound of music. Some one was playing on the old piano. There sat Miss Theodora. He saw her through a half-opened door, playing with a fervor that he could not have believed possible had he not seen it for himself. For a moment he watched her, and although he was not a learned young man, he thought at once of St. Cecilia.

There was, indeed, more than a mere suggestion of saintliness in Miss Theodora, with her pale face, with her black hair smoothly brushed away and gathered in a coil behind, and her patient expression.

"Why, Aunt Teddy," at length exclaimed Ernest, entering the room, "I didn't know that you were such a performer. I knew you could play, but I didn't know you could play like that."

"Thank you, Ernest," replied his aunt. "I don't play well now, but when your grandfather was living I had the very best instruction; but my style is so old-fashioned that I never play to any one now."

In truth, Miss Theodora had played well in her day, and it was one of the sorrows of her later life that she could not profit by the fine teachers and the concerts of music-loving Boston. Diantha, whose thirty years' devotion to the family gave her privileges, would

sometimes come to her as she sat alone
by the front window in the twilight, and
say:

"Why don't you never play no music
now, Miss Theodora?   I ain't forgot
how you used to practice all the time;
and Mr. John and Mr. William would
come into the parlor in the evenings and
listen to you, and you used to look so
pretty sitting at that very piano that you
won't never touch now."

Yet Ernest, although he had often
heard Diantha thus remonstrate with his
aunt, now first realized perhaps that
there was undue self-denial in his aunt's
life.   What Kate had said about "sacri-
fices" became significant to him.   With
as little delay as possible he would talk
with Richard Somerset.

XIV.

"Now, Ernest, I don't know what Theodora would do if she knew that I had told you, but since you insist I will say that your father left you nothing, absolutely nothing. He invested his small share of your grandfather's property badly, and when we came to settle things there wasn't a cent for you." So said Richard Somerset in the interview which Ernest soon sought.

"So all that I have is just that much less for Aunt Teddy?"

"Yes,—if you put it that way. But

she has told me many a time that whatever she has is yours. Just you do your
best at college, and become a clever lawyer like your father and your grandfather, and she'll be satisfied. You see,
you are all she has in the world. Of
course, if she had married,—" but here
the good man grew silent, and Ernest
never heard from him the story of Miss
Theodora's one love affair.

It was just as well that he stopped
where he did, for, with an indiscretion
worthy a younger man, he had already
gone far beyond Miss Theodora's in-
structions. He knew that it was her one
desire that Ernest should not learn that
he had no money of his own. When Ernest had heard the truth, much that pre-
viously he had not quite understood in
his aunt's management of affairs was explained.

"It's all very well to talk about being a
lawyer," he cried. "It's all very well to
talk; but I have found out that I cannot

possibly be one. It's been worrying me lately. Of course, I might go through college in a sort of way; but after what you tell me I can't see the sense in wasting time or money."

Richard Somerset looked aghast. Was this the effect of his words? What would Miss Theodora say?

"Why—why, you wouldn't disappoint your aunt like that, would you? What in the world would you do if you left college?"

"Well, I don't know exactly, but I'm pretty sure that I'd take a course like Ben Bruce has had at the Technology. Then I'd go West and make some money. One thing I've found out since I went to College,—and that is that I don't want to be poor the rest of my life."

"Everybody who goes West doesn't make money."

"Maybe not, but I met a man crossing on the Altruria this summer, who told me that mining engineers have the best possible chance now. He's a large stockholder in the 'Wampum and Etna,' and he said if only my profession were something in his line he could do a lot for me."

"Rather presuming for a stranger," said Richard Somerset, with the true Boston manner."

"He didn't seem like a stranger. He used to know my father, I believe. But he said it wasn't worth while to mention him to Aunt Theodora, as she probably wouldn't remember him."

"What was his name?"

"Easton—William Easton. I have his card and address somewhere. He used to be an army officer, captain of engineers, then he resigned and went into mining. He worked like everything until he made a lucky find. He was his own engineer for a time, but now he's given up active work. He and his wife go abroad every summer."

"No, it wasn't worth while to mention him to your aunt," said Richard Somerset, as Ernest left him. The older man gazed abstractedly after the boy, while his heart went out in sympathy with Miss Theodora.

Between Miss Theodora and William Easton there had once been an engagement, known only to their most intimate friends. John's classmate and comrade in the war, he had never concealed his admiration for John's sister. It was just after Dorothy's death, when Ernest demanded all Miss Theodora's time, that William Easton was ordered to the western frontier. With the reorganization of the army he had gone into the Engineers, and now there was no chance, had he wished, to evade the duty to which he was assigned. He might stay at his new post four or five years, he said, and Theodora must marry him and go too. Always imperative, he tried hard enough to carry his point. But for Ernest's claims Miss Theodora would have yielded.

"Ernest will come, too, of course," he said,—and failed, obstinately perhaps, to see the weight of Miss Theodora's objections. The locality to which he was bound was notoriously unhealthy. The surroundings would be in other respects unfavorable to the little boy,—and what chance would he have for an education in that remote and half-civilized region? Nor would Miss Theodora leave the child behind, even had there been any one with whom she could leave him. Surely she and William could wait. But William Easton, always impatient, went off to his distant post angry that Theodora should prefer a little child to him. Both were heart-sore at first, but time works wonders, and years after this parting, when Miss Theodora heard that he had married the daughter of a Colorado rancher, she hoped, yes, she really hoped, that he was happy.

Ernest did not recognize as William Easton, his steamboat acquaintance, the young officer who stood beside his father in the little faded photograph on his aunt's dressing table.   What queer, loose-fitting uniforms they had!   We'd smile if men wore their hair so long as that now."   This was all the boy had thought, as he looked at the picture. But for Miss Theodora these two faded figures symbolized her heart's whole history.

To keep Ernest from thinking much about money matters, Miss Theodora had discouraged intimacies with her richer distant relatives—excepting only the Digbys.   This one exception in the case of the Digbys needed no justification in her mind.   Had not Stuart been John's best friend?   Thus Ernest, growing up in the simple West End neighborhood, had little opportunity to make uncomfortable contrasts between his aunt's way of living and that of richer people.

Had Ralph and Ernest been more congenial, Ernest might have been drawn
into Ralph's set, made up of the boys of
his own age with the largest claims on
the so-called society of Boston.   As it
had been, Ralph and his friends formed
a little world apart from Ernest and his
interests.   With Ben as full confidant
and adviser, Ernest was naturally well
content with his own lot.   For Ben, with
so much less than Ernest had of the
things that money gives, was always
happy—apparently happy and absorbed
in his studies.   Ernest knew of course
that he himself must be economical,—his
aunt had often said so; but sometimes he
thought that this economy was only one
of her fancies,—she was so unlike other
people in many ways.   Especially probable did this seem when she gave him a
liberal allowance for Harvard.   He did
not know, until Richard Somerset told
him, that a bank failure a few years before had taken five thousand dollars of
Miss Theodora's small capital, and that

a mortgage of almost the same amount had been put on the house to enable her to carry out her plans for Ernest.

But Ernest's happy ignorance was now at an end. If his summer in Europe, his year in college, had done nothing else for him, these things had given him a desire for a larger life than he had had. Unless they take form in action desires of this kind may end in mere discontent, to eat into the heart of their possessor. Rightly directed, they will carry him along a path at the end of which, even if unsuccessful, he will at least have pleasure in remembering that he tried to reach a definite goal.

Thus Ernest, disturbed by the fact that his college course was less satisfactory to him than he had expected it to be, confronted by the knowledge that money, or lack of money, plays a large part in every-day affairs, overwhelmed by his discovery of the meagreness of his aunt's possessions, still hesitated a little as to his own duty.

XV.

Ernest's final decision was closely interwoven with a ride from Cambridge in an open horse-car one warm spring evening. Though his mind during this ride was constantly going over the subject that now lay near his heart, it afterward seemed to him as if he could recall every step of the way, so curiously sometimes does the external world weave itself into our mental processes. Long afterward he remembered that at first in the dim light he had noticed people, young and old, children or girls in light dresses, sitting on the piazzas or moving about the wide lawns of the houses near the Square. Next he saw the business blocks with their shops, in front of which groups of young men were lounging. Over-dressed girls and other young men promenaded the sidewalks in front of the shops, and he caught the occasional note of a loud laugh or a flippant remark. Farther on, rows of unpretentious dwellings, ending at last in unmistakable tenement houses, stamped themselves on his mind, with half-tidy women, men in their shirt sleeves, and little children crowding the doorways. Across the muddy flats and the broad river they might see, as he saw, the pretty hilly country beyond. Were they gossiping and scolding, much as they would gossip and scold in their narrow room? Perhaps for the time, like Ernest himself, they knew the peaceful influence of the perfect evening.

The indescribable May softness had, he felt sure, more than a little to do with his own exultation. His way opened perfectly clear before him. The arguments that he should use with his aunt stood out plainly defined. Go on longer as he had been doing!—he shivered at the thought.

Finding Miss Theodora alone in the twilight, he realized as never before the pathos of her lonely life. In saying what he was going to say he knew that he must shatter one of her cherished idols.

"In time, of course, she'll know that I have been right," he said to himself. Yet it required more than a little courage to speak, to argue with her against things that he knew she held so dear.

Though he hardly knew how it came about, the discussion ended, to Ernest's own surprise, with the advantage on his side. His skilful fashion of handling statistics told strongly in his favor, perhaps; for he proved to his aunt's satisfaction that it would be many, many years before he could probably support himself on a lawyer's income. He had figures and facts to show what he was certain to earn as soon as he began to practise engineering.

"But, Ernest," said Miss Theodora, "if you do not want to be a lawyer after you are graduated, there are many other things you might do without sacrificing your position in life." For although Miss Theodora knew well enough that mining engineers were not the same as the engineers whom she had seen on locomotives and steamboats, yet she felt that engineers in general, by reason of grimy hands and faces, were forever cut off from good society.

"What else can I find to do?" he insisted, "that would be as interesting and pay as well?"

"Well, I think that you could get into

the treasurer's office of the Nashawapag Mills.   Richard Somerset has great influence there."

"Now, Aunt Teddy, you wouldn't want me to be a book-keeper the rest of my life,—for that is all I'd be; and as for salary, unless I stayed there thirty or forty years, until those at the top died, I suppose that I could make a little more than a bare living, but it wouldn't be much more."

Then Miss Theodora, who could think of very few occupations outside of the learned professions in which a young man of good family might properly engage, at last surrendered to Ernest's arguments.

"We have so very little money," said Ernest, after he had let her know that Richard Somerset had told him how slight their resources were; "we are so poor, that in a few years I know that I would have to beg or borrow, and I'm sure you would not wish me to do one any more than the other."

"No, indeed," exclaimed his aunt.

"You see," he went on, "I am acquiring very extravagant tastes at Cambridge. There's no place like it for making you want money, if you once begin to contrast yourself with fellows who have plenty."

"But I thought you were independent," sighed poor Miss Theodora.

"Oh, I should be if I were really interested in my work," replied Ernest; "but, you see, I can't throw myself into my studies as I ought to."

It is to be feared that Ernest was worse than a little artful in thus painting himself as black as he could. He did not tell his aunt, what really was the truth, that it was harder for him to give up Harvard now than it would have been six months before. He had begun to have his own group of special friends; he had begun to enjoy many phases of college life. Despite certain distasteful studies, he might have gone through college without special discredit. He might have taken his degree, as many of his classmates would, with considerable culture and very little practical knowledge clinging to him. He trembled when he saw that he could take so kindly to dawdling ways. But his Puritan conscience interposed. When he knew how really poor they were, his love for his aunt and his pride all imparted to him a firmness at which he himself marvelled.

XVI.

Miss Theodora gave in, partly because she herself had begun to see that she might wrong Ernest by insisting on his carrying out her ideas. His poor rank in the classics showed a mind unlike that of his father or his grandfather. When she saw his brow darken at mention of the work he must do to get off his condition in Greek, she remembered how cheerful he had once been whistling over his work in his basement room. She longed to see him again engaged in congenial work or studies. Therefore, without vigorous defence, the castle in Spain which she had founded on Ernest's professional career fell under Ernest's direct assault. But she was disappointed, and although she did not go out of her way to look for sympathy, she accepted all that Miss Chatterwits and Diantha offered her. The former really believed that Harvard was the only institution in the United States in which a young man could get the higher education.

"I don't know," she said, "as I ever heard of a great man—that is, a scholar, for I don't forget some of the Presidents —that hadn't graduated at Harvard. Not but what a man might be great, I suppose, that wasn't what you would call a scholar; but I did think that Ernest would follow right after his grandfather, not to speak of his father. And all the books you've saved for him, too, Miss Theodora!—it does seem too bad."

"Oh, I still expect Ernest to be a great man," said Miss Theodora, a trifle dubiously. "I am sure that he has shown considerable talent already for inventing things."

"Ye-es," was Miss Chatterwits' doubtful response. "Ye-es,—but it seems as if most of the things has been invented that's at all likely to give a man a great reputation,—the telegraphs and steamboats and steam engines, not to mention sewing machines, which I must say has made a great difference in my work."

"Oh, well, sometimes men benefit the world by inventing some little thing, or making an improvement—well, in steam engines or something of that kind."

"I dare say,—I haven't any doubt but Ernest'll be smarter than any boy in the school where he's going. But it always did seem to me that studies of that kind were well enough for Ben Bruce—and such; but Ernest,—he seems to belong out at Harvard."

This was unkind—for Miss Chatterwits really liked Ben Bruce very much. But lately she had had one or two rather wordy encounters with Mrs. Bruce when they had met by chance at a neighbor's house. The little dressmaker was fond of "drawing the line," as she said, and relegating people, in conversation, at least, to their proper places. Mrs. Bruce had similar proclivities; but with less accurate data on which to base her classification of her neighbors, she sometimes made mistakes on which Miss Chatterwits was bound to frown.

"If I went about sewing from house to house," said Mrs. Bruce, "I suppose I might know more about people than I do; but being in private life, it isn't to be supposed I know much but what has been handed down to me in my own family."

"Well, if you went about sewing from house to house," said Miss Chatterwits, "you'd be more use to your family than you are now." With which last word Miss Chatterwits had flounced away, and for a time spoke somewhat depreciatingly of the Bruces, although in her heart she envied them their Revolutionary ancestor.

Miss Theodora had no petty pride. She liked Ben; she knew that he was a good friend for Ernest, and the one thing that reconciled her to the change in Ernest's career was the fact that, for a year at least, he would be able to have much help and advice from Ben. After the latter should get his scientific degree, he would probably leave Boston; but for the present she knew that his friendship would mean much to Ernest.

Ernest spent six weeks of the summer after his decision about college at a quiet seashore village with Ben. Ben tutored Ernest in various branches in which he was deficient, and proved an even better friend to him than Miss Theodora had hoped. Sometimes, as they sat in a little cove at the edge of the water, letting their books fall from their hands, gazing at the crescent-shaped Plymouth shore, they would talk of many things outside of their work. Ben was an enthusiast about the early history of New England.

He loved to theorize over the country's possibilities, and to trace its present greatness from the principles planted by the Plymouth and Massachusetts Bay colonies. Once as they sat there talking, Ernest exclaimed: "Those men were workers, Ben! Sometimes I think that we are all wrong today,—we attach so much importance to books. Now, I believe that I should have been much better off now and happier if I could have gone at once to work two or three years ago, instead of undertaking—"

But Ben interrupted him. "Oh, no! you are wrong. You do not realize your privileges. Perhaps you will be surprised to hear that I envied you your chance of going to Harvard. It would have been my choice to go there if I could. But the Institute was more practical, and I dare say was the best for me. Only—don't make too little account of your advantages, Ernest."

What Ben said was true enough. His

own mind was essentially that of the scholar. He could have gone on forever acquiring knowledge. He had no desire to put it at once to the practical use to which necessity compelled him. Yet, understanding Ernest's temperament, he had not discouraged him from leaving college, and he stood ready to help him to the utmost in his scientific work.

Many a time, however, with no envious mind, he had wished that it had been his to change places with Ernest. What delightful hours, he thought, he could have passed within the gray walls of the college library! He would have been no more inclined than Ernest, perhaps, to follow Miss Theodora's plans for a lawyer's career. No; he would have aimed rather to be a Harvard professor. Had fortune favored him, he would have spent a long time in post-graduate study, not only at Cambridge, but at some foreign university. "What folly!" he would then suddenly cry; "life is practical." But while doing the duty that lay nearest, he knew well enough that Harvard would have meant infinitely more to him than his chosen course.

During two years only of Ernest's Technology course were he and Ben together. When the latter was graduated he went West at once to begin his contest for the honors and the wealth which were to work that wonderful change in the affairs of his family. But Ernest had started well, and even without his friend's guidance he kept on in the path he had marked out. To give an account of the four years of his work would be to tell a rather monotonous story. This was not because he allowed his life to be a mere routine—far from this. While he worked energetically during the winter, he managed to find time for recreation. Society, so-called, did not interest him. But he had a group of friends, of fixed purpose like his own, who were still sufficiently boyish to enjoy life.

With them he took long walks in search of geological specimens, inviting them home on winter evenings to share Miss Theodora's simple tea.

From some of these Western friends of Ernest's, with a point of view so unlike her own, Miss Theodora gained an entirely different outlook on life. Ernest had impressed on her the fact that the West was to be his home, at least, until he had made a lot of money. She began, therefore, to take an interest, not only in these Westerners, with their broad pronunciation, but in the Western country itself. She re-read "The Oregon Trail"; she read one or two other books of Western travel. She studied the topography of Colorado and Nevada in her old atlas, and she always noted in the newspapers chance scraps of information about that distant region.

Nahant knew Ernest no more in summer. His long vacation was always spent elsewhere in practical field work.

He almost dropped out of the lives of
those who had known him so well as a
little boy.   At the same time, he had
enough social diversion.   In the new set
of which he now formed one there was
always more or less going on.   The sisters of some of his friends invited him to
their dances.   He seemed so heartily to
enjoy his new popularity that Kate realized, with a certain pain, that he was
drawing away from her; that he was de-
parting far from that pleasant old West
End life.   There was an irony of fate in
remembering that by using her influence
in the direction of the new work which
Ernest had undertaken, she had helped
to send him farther away.

XVII.

When the die was finally cast, Miss Theodora wisely kept to herself her disappointment at Ernest's change of plan. Her life thus far had accustomed her to disappointments. What a pang she had felt, for example, some years after leaving it, when she heard that the old family house on the hill had become a boarding house! How disturbed she had been, walking up Beacon Street one day, to see workmen tearing down one of the most dignified of the old purple-windowed houses, once the home of intimate friends of hers, to make way for an uglier if more ornate structure! What an intrusion she felt the car tracks to be which run through Charles Street across Beacon Street, connecting the South and the West Ends of the city! Miss Theodora's Boston was not so large but that it could be traversed by any healthy person on foot; and she agreed with Miss Chatterwits when she exclaimed, "What in the world has the West End to do with Roxbury Neck?"

Real trials, like Ernest's change of plan, Miss Theodora was able to bear with surprising equanimity. She had not even quailed when she made that discovery, hardest of all even for a sensible woman, that she was growing old. The first rude shock had come one day in a horse-car, when she heard an overdressed young mother say to her little

son in a loud whisper: "Give the old lady
a seat." Before this Miss Theodora had
certainly not thought of herself as old;
but looking in the glass on her return
home, she saw that the youth had vanished from her face. For though the
over-dressed young mother might have
said "oldish"more truly than "old," yet
Miss Theodora realized that the change
had come.

What it was she could scarcely define,
save that there were now long lines on
her cheek where once there had been
curves, that her eyes were perhaps less
bright, that gray hairs had begun to appear, and that certainly she had less color
than formerly. All these changes had
not come in a day, and yet in a day, in
an hour, Miss Theodora realized them.
As she looked in the mirror and saw that
her gray hairs were still few enough to
count, she glanced below the glass to the
little faded photograph on the table.
John had passed into the land of per-

petual youth, and William, that other, had he begun to show the marks of age?

Thus she wondered as she gazed at the young man with the longish, thick hair, at which Ernest had sometimes laughed. But she seldom let her mind wander in this direction, and she turned it now toward other friends of her girl-hood, of whom some occasionally flitted across her vision. The most of those who had been her contemporaries the winter she came out were now married. Of these, she could not recall one who had not "married well," as the phrase is. Were they growing old more gracefully than she? Would she change places with any one of those portly matrons, absorbed now in family or social inter-ests? The sphere of the unmarried few was unattractive to her. The causes, whether literary or philanthropic, into which the majority threw themselves had certainly no charm for her. She could not have worked for the Indians after the

manner of her cousin Sarah Somerset.
To her the Indian race seemed too cruel
for the enthusiasm lavished on it by a
certain group of Boston women.

When her father had verged toward
Transcendentalism she had lagged behind, and more modern "isms" were even
farther out of her reach. She listened
dubiously to rhapsodies by one of her
cousins on the immense spiritual value
of the Vedas. Woman suffrage! Well,
she had only one friend who waxed eloquent over this, and Miss Theodora, although on the whole liberal-minded, was
repelled from a study of the question by
the peculiarities of dress and manner affected by some of its devotees. Even
Culture itself, with a capital letter, and
all that this implies could never have
been a fad of hers. The books people
talked about now were so different from
those that she had been accustomed to;
she knew nothing about modern French
literature, and her friends cared nothing

for Miss Ferrier or Crabbe. After all, Miss Theodora would not have changed places with one of these friends of her youth, married or unmarried, with their tablets covered with social engagements or note-books crammed with appointments for meetings or lectures. She found her own life sufficiently full.

That she was growing old brought her little worry, coming as it did at the same time with the change in Ernest's plans. Although she would have been very slow to admit it, Kate's thorough approval of Ernest's new career modified Miss Theodora's own view of it. Unconsciously she had begun to dream of a united fortune for Kate and Ernest; for in her eyes the two were perfectly adapted to each other.

"There's a prospect of your amounting to something now," she heard Kate say to Ernest one day. "You haven't been at all like yourself this winter, and I just believe that college would have ruined you," she continued frankly.

It was Kate who pointed out to Miss Theodora the perils that surrounded a young man who was not very much interested in his work at Cambridge.

"Well, of course you ought to know, for you have a brother in college."

"Oh, dear me, Ernest and Ralph aren't a bit alike. Ernest would always be different from Ralph, I should hope." For Kate and Ralph, since their childhood, had gone on very different paths.

"No, I'm not afraid of Ernest's growing like Ralph; but I know that Ernest is more easily influenced than you think, and it's a good thing that he's going to have studies that will interest him." All of which seemed to Miss Theodora to augur well for the plans which she had formed for these two young people.

To Ernest Kate spoke even more frankly than to his aunt. "I knew that you'd do it," she said, "and I feel almost sure that you'll make a great man, and really you will be able to help your aunt much sooner than if you began to study law. As soon as possible I want Cousin Theodora to have lots of money. She won't accept anything from me, and you have no idea how many things there are that she needs money for."

So Ernest, encouraged by the good opinion of the young woman he cared most for, made less than he might have made of the older woman's disappointment. He made less of it, perhaps, because, with the confidence of youth, he believed the time near when she would admit that he had done the very best thing for them both.

XVIII.

Mrs. Fetchum pressed her face close to the window pane to watch Miss Theodora enter her door.

"It seems to me Miss Theodora ain't quite as firm on her feet as she used to be. Don't you think she stoops some?" she said to her husband.

"Miss Theodora's getting along," was the answer. "She's not as young as she was."

"She isn't older than Mrs. Stuart Digby, but she's had a sight more care. Well, speaking of angels, there she is now,"—and the good woman's voice trembled with excitement as Mrs. Digby's victoria drew up before Miss Theodora's door.

From time to time Mrs. Digby's horses scornfully pawed the pavement in front of Miss Theodora's house, while the owner waited for her cousin to get ready for the drive.   Miss Theodora never greatly enjoyed these drives, for a certain condescension in Mrs. Digby's manner always disturbed her.   She knew, too, that she was seldom invited unless the latter had some object of her own to serve.   On the present occasion they were hardly seated in the carriage before the special purpose of this drive was revealed.

"Kate is a great trial to me, Theodora. Would you believe, I can't get her to take the least interest in society?   Why, I couldn't make her go to the cotillions this winter.   With her bright manner she would be very popular; and it's too provoking to think, after all the advantages she's had, she fairly throws herself away on old ladies and colored children, —and I do wish that you'd help me."

Miss Theodora trembled as if guilty herself of some misdeed. "What can I do?" she asked faintly, knowing well enough that it was she who had interesed Kate in the Old Ladies' Home and the colored children.

Mrs. Digby seemed to read her thoughts. "Of course, I don't want her to give up her reading to the old ladies altogether. But I do wish you could make her realize her obligations to society. I can't myself. Why, she refuses all invitations, and hardly ever goes even to her sewing circle. The next thing she'll be taking vows at St. Margaret's or doing something equally absurd."

Miss Theodora, though aware of the hopelessness of so doing, promised to use her influence with Kate.

Mrs. Digby herself was born for society, and it was a trial even greater than she had represented to Miss Theodora that her daughter should be so indifferent to the great world.

"Kate has style," she said to her cousin, "and manner, and if she only would exert herself to please my friends to the extent that she exerts herself to please nobodies, I should have little to complain of. Poor Stuart's death was very unfortunate, happening just the winter Kate was ready to come out. It put an end, of course, to all the plans I had made for her among the younger set. She didn't mind missing balls and parties herself, for she never cared for that kind of thing; but I do think, now that she is out of mourning, that she might take a little interest in society, and at least accept some of the dinner invitations she has."

"But she does go out a good deal, doesn't she?" began Miss Theodora, remembering some of Kate's humorous accounts of amusing episodes connected with various little dinner parties she had attended.

"Oh, yes; I often insist on her going with me; and once in a while there is some invitation she really wishes to accept. But it is the duty of a girl of her age to be seen more in society; and I do wish that she could be made to understand that she owes something to her position and to her family."

"Well, I will speak to her," said Miss Theodora, "but I doubt if I can influence her to any great extent."

"Indeed you can," responded Mrs. Digby. "You know how I feel, I am sure. I don't want Kate to be an old maid, and she's older now than I was when I married. Thus far, she has not had the slightest interest in any young man, although she has plenty of admirers. Perhaps I ought to be thankful for this, for it would be just in line with her general perversity for her to fall in love

with some thoroughly unsuitable person."

Possibly Miss Theodora, with Ernest
ever in mind, was unusually sensitive in
detecting undue emphasis in Mrs.
Digby's pronunciation of "any" when
she said that Kate had not the "slightest
interest in any young man." Or perhaps Mrs. Digby, too, had Ernest in
mind when she made this sweeping
statement.

Two people could hardly be more unlike than Kate and her mother. Mrs.
Digby was of dark complexion, of com-
manding figure, though not over tall,
and she lived for society. Kate was
blond, with a half-timid, though
straightforward air, and she was as anxious to keep far from the whirl of things
as her mother was to be active in her
little set. Mrs. Digby had worn heavy
mourning for her husband the exact
length of time demanded by strict pro-
priety. But just as soon as she could,

she laid aside her veil and, indeed, crepe in every form, and gave outer shape to her grief by clothing herself in becoming black relieved by abundant trimmings of dull jet.

"I could wish Mrs. Digby no worse punishment," said one of her intimate enemies, "than to be condemned to attend a round of dinners in a high-necked gown." From which it might truly be inferred that Mrs. Digby herself was thought to have no mean opinion of Mrs. Digby arrayed in conventional dinner attire. Yet her most becoming low-necked gown Mrs. Digby could have given up almost more readily than the dinners which she had to sacrifice in her year of mourning. She had been fond of her husband, no one could deny that. But, after all, she missed him less than the outside world thought she missed him. He and she had led decidedly separate lives for many years before his death, and, indeed, in the early years the stress of feeling had been more on his side than on hers. She was not long, therefore, in returning to a round of gayety, somewhat subdued, to be sure, but still "something to take me away from myself and my grief," she occasionally said half-apologetically to those who, like Miss Theodora, she knew must be surprised at her return to the world. On this particular occasion, after making her request for Miss Theodora's influence with Kate, she continued:

"If it were not for Ralph I do not know what I should do. He goes everywhere with me, and is perfectly devoted to society. Now, in his case, I almost hope he won't marry. I should hate to give him up to any one else. But he is so fastidious that I know it will be some time before he settles upon any one,—although I must say that he is a great favorite.

This was the early autumn after

Ralph's graduation. He had gone through Harvard very creditably, and had even had honorable mention in history and modern languages. Mrs. Digby, however, with all her pride in her son, felt that the large income which he drew went for other than legitimate college expenses. As a woman of the world, she said that Ralph could not be so very unlike the men who were his associates, and she knew that certain rumors about them and their doings could not be wholly false. Nevertheless, she seldom reproved her son, and she even took pride in his self-possessed and ultra-worldly manner. Surely that kind of thing was infinitely better form than Kate's self-consciousness and Puritan frankness.

Mrs. Digby graced a victoria even more truly than she graced a low-necked gown. Indeed, to the many who, never having had the good fortune to see her in a drawing-room, knew her only by name and sight as she rolled through the streets, she and the victoria seemed inseparable, a kind of modernized centaur. It was impossible for such people to think of her in any other attitude than that of haughty semi-erectness on the ample cushions of her carriage.

On this particular day, as Mrs. Digby drove down Beacon Street, and thence by the river over the Milldam, she met many friends and bowed to them.

"Who in the world has Mrs. Digby got with her today?" some of them would ask their companions, in the easy colloquialism of every-day life.

"I haven't the faintest idea, but she's a rather out-of-date-looking old person," was the usual reply, although occasionally some one would identify Miss Theodora, usually adding: "I knew her when she was a girl, but she's certainly very much changed. Well, that's what comes of living out of the world."

These drives with Mrs. Digby always made Miss Theodora feel her own lone-

liness. In this city—this Boston—
which had always been her own home
and the home of her family, she had few
friends. She could hardly have known
fewer people if living in a foreign city.
It was therefore with a start of relief that
she heard Mrs. Digby exclaim:

"Why, there's Ernest, isn't it?"

Miss Theodora glanced ahead. Near-
sighted though she was, she had no
trouble in recognizing her nephew's
broad shoulders and swinging gait. But
the young man was not alone. He was
walking rather slowly, and bending toward a girl in a close-fitting tailor-made
suit. It was the end of October, too
early for furs, yet the girl was anticipat-
ing the winter fashions. One end of a
long fuzzy boa flaunted itself over her
shoulder, stirred, like the heavy ostrich
plumes in her hat, by the afternoon
breeze.

. "It isn't Kate, is it?" said Miss Theodora, dubiously, as the carriage drew
near the pair.

"No, indeed, not Kate," quickly answered Mrs. Digby.

"I wonder who it can be," continued Miss Theodora, for she could not help observing Ernest's tender air toward the girl.

"Oh, I'm sure I can't say, Theodora. It's certainly no one I know; but Kate—or perhaps it was Ralph—has been saying something about a flirtation of Ernest's with some girl he met somewhere last year." Then seeing that Miss Theodora looked downcast: "Oh, it isn't likely it's anything serious, Theodora; it's only what you must expect at his age, and of course his interests are all so different now from what you had expected, that it isn't surprising to find him flirting or falling in love with girls whom you and I know nothing about."

By this time the carriage had passed the two young people, and Ernest was so absorbed in his companion that he did not even see it rolling by.

XIX.

Poor Miss Theodora! One walk on a public thoroughfare with a girl heretofore unknown to one's relatives need not imply the surrender of a young man's affections; but Ernest, so his aunt thought, was not like other young men. He would be sincere in a matter of this kind. If his interest in any girl had been so marked as to be a subject of comment for Ralph and Kate, it must be known to many other people. Yet why had Kate not spoken to her, as well as to her mother; or why had not Ernest himself suggested the direction in which his fancy was wandering? Many questions like these crowded Miss Theodora's mind, for which she had no satisfactory answer. Strangest of all,—and she could hardly account for her own reticence,—she said not a word to Kate nor to Ernest of all this that lay so near her heart. If Ben had been at home, she might have talked freely to him. He could have told whether or not Mrs. Digby's surmises were correct. But Ben had been in the West for a year and a half. If he had been at home, she thought, perhaps this would never have happened. Yet, after all, what was the "this" which so disturbed Miss Theodora's usually calm mind? What were the signs by which she recognized that Ernest had secrets which he did not confide to her?

The signs, though few, to her were positive. Ernest had begun to take

more interest in society. While studying diligently, he also found time for
more or less gayety. In the left-hand
corner of his top bureau drawer there
was·a heap of dance programmes and
progressive euchre tally-cards. Kate
had seen.them one day when helping
Miss Theodora put Ernest's room in
order. She had given a scornful "No"
when the former asked her if she had
been at a dance whose date was indi-
cated on a certain programme.

"Of course, I know you seldom go to
dances, but still I thought perhaps—"

"Oh, Cousin Theodora, I haven't
been at a dance this winter; and as to
these parties that Ernest has been going
to — there was a set of them, wasn't
there? I really don't recognize the
names of any of the managers."

Now this reply was not reassuring to
Miss Theodora, who had a vague hope
that Kate and Ernest met occasionally
in society. Then Kate continued:

"Ernest is really growing very giddy.
Just look at that heap of neckties. I
should say some of them had not been
worn twice, and then he has flung them
down as if he didn't intend to wear them
again."

Now in the midst of her railing, Kate
stopped. In the back of the drawer, behind the neckties, she had caught sight
of a photograph,—it was the face of a
girl she had seen before,—and she
closed the drawer with a snap that made
Miss Theodora look up quickly from her
task of dusting the books on Ernest's
study table. Just then Diantha passed
the door.

"I've been telling Miss Theodora," she
cried, with the familiarity of an old servant, "I've been telling Miss Theodora
that I believe Mast' Ernest's in love. He
don't spend much time with us now, and
I reckon 'tain't study that takes him out
every evening. I shouldn't wonder if
you knows more about it than we do,"—

and Diantha rolled her large eyes significantly at Kate.

But Kate was silent, and Miss Theodora was silent, and Diantha, with a toss of the head and arms akimbo, passed on to her little attic room. Nor when she was gone did the two ladies speak to each other of the thing which lay so near their hearts.

Now, Miss Theodora, until driven thereto by Mrs. Digby, had never contemplated the possibilty of Ernest's taking a tender interest in any one not approved by her. She had never resented Sarah Fetchum's addressing him by his first name, even after he had entered college and Sarah herself was almost through the Normal School. She could invite Sarah and her intimate friend, Estelle Tibbits, to take tea with her without any fear that Ernest would fall in love with either of them.

Unaware, apparently, of his aunt's solicitude, Ernest continued to mix a little

play with the hard work of his last year
of study.   Miss Theodora, at least, had
no reason to complain of neglect from
him.   He went with her to the Old
West Church on Sunday morning as
willingly as ever he had gone in the days
of his childhood.   Indeed, as a little boy
she had often had to urge him unduly to
go with her, and sometimes he would try
to beg off with the well-worn plea that
he "hated sermons."   Later, as they sat
in the high-backed pew which they
shared with the Somersets, Miss Theodora would notice the boy's fair head
moving restlessly from side to side.

As years passed on Ernest grew as
fond as his aunt of the old church, with
its plain white ceiling and gallery, sup-
ported by simple columns, and its tablets in honor of men of a bygone age.
If sometimes on Sunday afternoons he
went to Trinity Church, contented to
stand for an hour in the crowded aisle
to hear the uplifting words of the great

preacher, he never made this later service an excuse for neglecting his aunt's
church. In this, as in almost all other
matters in which she had marked prefer-
ences, Ernest gave Miss Theodora little
ground for complaint.

Toward the end of his Technology
course Ernest made all his other interests bend to study. No longer had he
any evening engagements to worry his
aunt. He read late into the night. His
thesis occupied most of his day, for it
involved an immense amount of practical work in a factory out of town. As
Miss Theodora observed his zeal, as she
heard reports of his good standing in his
class, she could but contrast this state of
affairs with his unsatisfactory year at
Harvard.

XX.

"Isn't it perfectly splendid?" cried Kate, who, in spite of a general precision of speech, was not above using an occasional superlative. Miss Theodora had been less than human had she contradicted her young cousin, whose words referred to Ernest's thesis. For, although it bristled with scientific terms which they understood hardly as well as the majority of his auditors, Miss Theodora and Kate listened eagerly to every word. "Of course, you're proud of him; now you can't say you're not;"— and the young girl gave her cousin's hand a squeeze which the elder woman returned with interest. That his relatives were not partial was proved by the newspapers the next morning, for they made especial mention of Ernest, and said that he seemed likely to add new honors to the distinguished name he bore. Though Miss Theodora would have preferred to see Ernest in flowing gown on the Sanders Theatre platform, with the Governor and his staff and distinguished professors and noted alumni in the background, she did not express her regrets to Kate. A Harvard Commencement is unlike any other, and Kate, who realized this as strongly almost as Miss Theodora did, whispered, "Please don't think you're sorry that it isn't a Harvard A. B."

How could any one who loved him be otherwise than happy to see Ernest in so cheerful a mood, smiling at his aunt and Kate, bowing to Miss Chatterwits, who had a good seat near the front? If only he had not rushed up in one of the intermissions to speak to that piquant-looking girl in the large white hat, whom Kate from a distance regarded with an air of interest mixed with disdain.

After the excitement of this last day, Ernest, contrary to his usual habit, was moody and restless. Miss Theodora watched him narrowly. She had hoped when the pressure of work was removed that he would settle down into calm ways, and put off as long as possible the inevitable decision about his future career. Must he, she wondered, must he really go to that great indefinite West, which years before had seemed the grave of a large share of her happiness?"

Ernest himself soon put an end to her wondering.

"Come, Aunt Teddy," he said one morning, drawing her beside him on the massive sofa that faced the bookcase, with its rows of neglected law books; "let us talk over my future. How soon can I go? I am lounging about here too long."

"Go?" she queried. "Go where?"— though in her heart she knew very well.

"Now don't equivocate; it isn't natural for you, Aunt Theodora; you are generally so straightforward. Don't you remember that I told you that I might have a good offer to go to Colorado? Well, it has come."

Whereupon Ernest proceeded to read a letter offering him a definite position and a stated salary with a certain mining company, and the letter was signed "William Easton."

"Isn't it fine to have such a chance?"

said the young man, looking up, and noting a surprising change in his aunt's face. She had grown extremely pale, and he saw that she was trembling.

"William Easton," she said, without answering his question; "how strange!"

Then there flashed across Ernest's mind his cousin Richard's warning against mentioning Mr. Easton to his aunt. Of course, the time for silence on this point had now passed,—and he continued:

"Yes; perhaps I may not have mentioned Mr. Easton's name before; but I didn't know that you would recall it. You've heard me speak of him, of course, the president of the Wampum and Etna, whom I met on the Altruria. He's as good as his word, and though I haven't heard from him for two years, here's this letter offering me the very chance he said he would give me—all on account of my father, I suppose. They must have been greater friends than I thought,"—looking questioningly toward Miss Theodora.

"Yes, they were great friends," answered she, "and I knew him very well too, but I would almost rather not have you accept his offer."

"Just because I shall have to go so far away, I suppose. Now, what else would you have me do?"

"Surely there are other chances in Boston. You can find something to do here."

"If I could, I wouldn't," replied the young man. "Now, what would be the sense in staying here? Of course, I could get something to do, there's no doubt of that; but it would be wicked to refuse an offer like this."

"Why not begin here and gradually work up? We don't need so very much money, Ernest —"

"Oh, Aunt Teddy, I do. What would you say if I told you I thought of getting married?"

"You—you—get married!" and Miss Theodora actually blushed. Then recollecting herself, "I am delighted," she said. "Kate is a dear girl. Not a bit like her mother."

"Kate! It isn't Kate," stammered the young man; and Miss Theodora, with a sudden revulsion of feeling, recalled many things that she had almost forgotten. Much that she had not understood was now explained. There was somebody, after all, whom Ernest cared for—and it wasn't Kate.

"Who is the young lady?" she asked with some dignity.

"Why, Eugenie. Haven't you heard me speak of Eugenie Kurtz?"

Miss Theodora shook her head.

"Of course," he said, "it isn't an engagement, or I would have told you all about it or asked your advice, but it's all so uncertain. Her father —"

"Who is her father?" asked Miss Theodora. "The name sounds familiar."

"Of course—you've seen it on his wagons, and I daresay you've been in his shop, too. He's really the chief man in the firm, for, although his partner's name stands first, Mr. Kurtz has really bought Brown out, all but a small share."

Then Miss Theodora remembered one of the best known retail shops in the city, whose growth from small beginnings was often quoted as a striking example of American energy. She remembered, too, that one partner—perhaps both—had been referred to as of humble origin. This remembrance came to her in a flash, and she took up Ernest's last words:

"Her father —"

"Yes, her father," repeated the young man, "won't consent to an engagement at present. I've got to show what I can do in the world, and so I must go West, where I can have room enough to move around." And then Ernest digressed into praise of Eugenie, her charms of person and manner, her taste in dress, her ability in housekeeping, in which she had had much experience since her mother's death. "You will call on her, won't you?" he pleaded.

But Miss Theodora would say neither yes nor no, as he named the street where Eugenie lived.   She knew this street very well.   She had passed through it several times in the evenings with Ernest.   She had never liked it, this long, new street, with its blocks of handsome bay-windowed houses.   How seldom were the curtains in these bay-windows drawn close!   She could not think well of people who left their rooms thus immodestly exposed to the gaze of passersby.   Brought up as she had been to regard lamp-light as a signal for the closing of blinds and curtains, she always turned her head away from the windows revealing beyond the daintily shaded lamp a glimpse of rooms furnished much more gorgeously than any to which she was accustomed. These unshaded windows had always seemed to her typical of the lives, of the minds, of the dwellers in the bay-windowed houses—no retirement, no privacy, all show.

To think that Ernest's interests should have begun to mingle with those of people whom she could never, never care to know! Miss Theodora sighed. Perhaps it was the best thing after all for Ernest to go West. Absence might make him forget Eugenie. "At his age," thought Miss Theodora, "it is ridiculous for him to imagine himself in love."

Yet Ernest, though Miss Theodora knew it not, had been deeply in love more than once before. There was that beautiful creature with the reddish-brown hair—several years older than he, to be sure—whom he had met on his passage back from Europe. What a joy it had been to walk the deck with her, while she confided all her past and present sorrows to him! He did not tell her his feelings then — she might have laughed at him. Later, how his heart had palpitated as he crossed the little square, past the diminutive statues of Columbus and Aristides, to call on her at the home of the sisterhood where she thought of taking vows! How well she looked in the severe garb of the order! so saintly, indeed, did she appear as she swept into the bare room, that he made only a short call, recrossing the square more in love than ever, though in a sombre mood.

A few months after, when he heard of the would-be devotee's marriage to old Abram Tinker, that crabbed millionaire, he was surprised to find himself so little disturbed. His happy disposition gave cynicism no place even for a foothold, and soon he barely remembered this little episode in his life. Eugenie, indeed, seemed to him the only woman he had ever cared for. He longed to talk about her to Kate, but something prevented his opening his heart to the latter. Nor was his aunt ready to listen to him. He was amazed to find her so unsympathetic. Her opposition to his going to the West had, however, disappeared. She even hastened his preparations, and bade him good-bye at the last with unexpected cheerfulness.

XXI.

Ernest, travelling West, had plenty of time to wonder if, after all, the present satisfied him. His answer on the whole was "yes." He had little to regret in the past; he was hopeful, he was positive about the future. A classmate travelled with him as far as Chicago, and this part of the journey, broken by a few hours' stay at Niagara, seemed short enough. Chicago itself, with its general air of

business bustle and activity, opened a
new world to him.   At the head office
of the Wampum and Etna, where letters
awaited him from Mr. Easton, he found
himself at once a man of consequence—
no longer the student, little more than
schoolboy, that he had been so lately in
the eyes of most persons.   Here the
clerks in the office bowed deferentially;
the agent consulted him; evidently Mr.
Easton intended to give him much re-
sponsibility.

In his day or two in the great city he
drove or walked in the parks, through
the boulevards, and along the lake front.
He grasped, as well as he could in so
short a time, the city's vastness, meas-
ured not alone by extent of territory, by
height of buildings, but by resources,
the amount of which he gathered from
the fragments of talk that came to him
in his hurried interviews with various
business men.   Boston, looked at with
their eyes, through the large end of the

telescope, was almost lost in a dwindling perspective. The West End,—how trivial all its interests! Miss Theodora, Kate, Miss Chatterwits, Diantha,—well, these loomed up a little larger than the city itself; and Eugenie—ah! she filled the field of the telescope, until Ernest could see little else.

After he had crossed the fertile fields of Illinois, and had watched the green farms of Nebraska fade away into the dull brown, uncultivated plains, he grew lonely, realizing how far he was from all that was dearest to him. Would not Miss Theodora's heart have ached with a pain deeper than that caused by this separation, could she have known that all her years of devotion were obscured by the glamor of that one bright year in which Ernest had felt sure of Eugenie's love.

As he looked from the car window across the wide stretch of open country, where the only objects between his eye

and the distant horizon were a canvas-
covered wagon or a solitary horseman,
Ernest had more than enough time for
reflection. Would Eugenie be true to
him? Of course; surely that was not a
doubt tugging at his heart-strings.
Would her father be more reasonable?
His brow darkened a little as he thought
of his last interview with Mr. Kurtz.

"No," the latter had said decidedly;
"it is not worth while to talk of an engagement. Time enough for that when
you have shown what you can do. As I
understand it, you have no special prospects at present. At least, it's to be
proved whether you'll succeed in the
West. I've known a good many people
to fail out there. I can't have Eugenie
bound by an indefinite engagement.
I've worked hard for her, and she's used
to everything. What could you give
her? If Eugenie married tomorrow,
she'd want just as much as she has to-
day. She isn't the kind of a girl to live

on nothing but love. I've talked with her, and know how she feels."

This last sentence had made Ernest shiver, and now, as it recurred to him, he again wondered if, after all, Eugenie was less in earnest than he.

He recalled the dignity with which Mr. Kurtz had drawn himself up as he said:

"Besides, I'm not going to have Eugenie go into a family likely to look down on her." Then, paying no attention to Ernest's protests, "Oh, yes, I know what I'm talking about. I haven't done business in Boston for nothing these forty years without knowing what they call the difference between people. It isn't much more than skin deep, but they feel it, all your people. I'm a self-made man, and I'm not ashamed of it. I don't ask any favors of any one, and I don't want any—and I'm not anxious to have my daughter go among people who will look down on her."

"But my people are so few," poor Ernest had said. "My aunt —"

"Oh, your aunt—yes—people respect her, and she's very good to the poor; but she was born in Boston, and she don't believe in marrying out of her set any more than if she was a Hindoo—unless she's made different from most Boston men and women. I know that I'm made of the same flesh and blood as the rest of them. But then I wasn't born in Boston, and perhaps my eyesight is clearer on that account. At any rate, I'm going to do my duty by Eugenie."

Then Ernest, reflecting on this conversation, from which he had gleaned so little comfort, fell asleep, and when he awoke in the morning they were not so very far from Denver. Far, far ahead, across the great plateau, an irregular dark line showed clear against the morning sky. "The Rockies," some one cried, and then he felt half like crying, half like turning back. His new life had almost begun, and he was hardly ready for it.

Could Ernest have known Mr. Kurtz's true state of mind, he would have had less reason for downheartedness. Eugenie's father saw in the young man more promise than he cared to express. He liked Ernest's frankness in speaking of his prospects; and he knew that he was no fortune hunter.

By her friends Eugenie was called the most "stylish" girl of her set. Always sure to be the leader's partner at the numerous Germans which were then so in vogue, she was certainly popular. With no wish ungratified by her father, she might have been more selfish than she was. It is true that she always had her own way, but then, as she said, when her father complained of this, "My own way is just as apt to benefit other people as myself." Without planning any beneficences, she did many little kindnesses to her friends. She had to have a companion when she went to Europe, and so, although a chaperone had been already provided, Mr. Kurtz cheerfully paid the expenses of a girl friend of hers, who otherwise would have been unable to go; and many other similar things added to her popularity.

After a year at a finishing school in New York, she had returned home, to find out that popularity in a small set is not everything. Some persons said that a desire to climb had led her to single out Ernest for especial favor. His name would be an open sesame to a great many Boston doors.

The little circles of rich, self-made men, self-satisfied women in which she moved did not touch that one in which she knew Ernest rightfully belonged. When, innocently enough, Ernest would speak of some invitation he had received, or would mention familiarly some one whose name for her had a kind of sacredness, all this was like a drop from Tantalus' cup for poor Eugenie.

But Ernest, measuring himself by his lack rather than by his possessions, never associated worldliness with Eugenie. He was captivated by her beauty, by her vivacity, by her brilliancy in repartee—Miss Theodora would have called the last "pertness." She spoke to him of his aunt, whom she knew by sight, wished that she might know her, and asked more about Kate Digby, who, Ernest said, was just like a sister to him.

"I should like to meet her," said Eugenie; and Ernest, before he left the city, had asked Kate to call on her.

A curious expression, which he could not quite read, came over Kate's face as she replied, "Really, I don't believe I can, Ernest; I haven't time enough now to call on half the girls I know. There are a dozen sewing circle calls that I've owed for a year, and it wouldn't be worth while to begin with any new people."

Nor, with all his attempts at persuasion, could Ernest get Miss Theodora to take the least interest in Eugenie.

"You know what I think about the whole matter," she said. "I won't dwell on my disappointment, but it will be time enough for me to know her when you are really engaged."

What wonder that Ernest, nearing Denver, felt disheartened, oppressed by his aunt's opposition, and the indefiniteness of his relations with Eugenie.

XXII.

Miss Theodora watered the morning-glories in the little yard behind the house with sighs, if not with tears. It was a poor little garden, this spot of greenery in the desert of back yards on which her windows looked. The flowers which she cultivated were neither many nor rare. Nasturtiums, sweet peas and morning-glories were dexterously trained to hide the ugliness of the bare brown fence. She had a number of hardy geraniums and a few low-growing things between the geraniums and the border of mignonette which edged the long, narrow garden bed. In one corner of the yard there was the dead trunk of a pear tree, whose crookedness Miss Theodora had tried to hide by trying to make a quick-growing vine climb over it. Curiously enough, all these attempts had been unsuccessful, and Ernest, commenting thereon, had said, laughingly:

"Why, yes, Aunt Theodora, that stump is so ugly that not even the kitten will climb over it."

Neverthless, there had been a time when the tree was full of leaves, and Miss Theodora, glancing at it now, a month after her nephew's departure, sighed, as she recalled how Ernest and Kate had loved to sit in its shade. Sometimes they had played shop there, when Ernest was always the clerk and Kate the buyer; but more often they had sat quietly on warm spring afternoons, while Ernest read and Kate cut out

paper dolls from the fashion plates of an
old magazine. Indeed, there were few
things in the house or out of it that did
not remind Miss Theodora of these two
young people. How could she bear it,
then, that their paths were to lie entirely
apart?

Did Kate feel aggrieved at Ernest's
attachment to "that girl," as Miss Theodora always characterized Eugenie?
She wondered if she herself had been too
stern in her attitude toward Ernest's
love affair. She had not been severe
with Ernest,—she deserved credit for
that, she said to herself,—yet she recalled with a pang his expression of dis-
may when she had said, "Really, Ernest,
you cannot expect me to call on Miss—
Miss Kurtz; at least, not at present."

She had excused herself by reflecting
that he was not old enough to decide in
a matter of this kind. It was very different from letting him choose his own
profession,—though she was beginning

to think that even in this matter she had made a mistake. If he had stayed at Cambridge he might never have met Eugenie Kurtz.

She had yielded to Ernest in the former case largely from a belief, founded on many years' observation, that half the unhappiness of middle life comes from the wrong choice of a career. She had seen men of the student temperament ground down to business, and regretting the early days when they might have started on a different path. She had noticed lawyers and clergymen who were better fitted to sell goods over a counter, and she had begun to think that medicine was the only profession which put the right man in the right place. This had influenced her in letting Ernest choose his own career.

But now, surely the time had come for her to be firm. Marriage—other mistakes might be rectified, but you could never undo the mischief caused by an ill-considered marriage. Oh, how happy she mgiht have been, if only Ernest and Kate were to be married. Well, it was not too late yet, and it seemed more than probable that her own stern attitude might help to bring about the desired result—a breaking off of his attachment to "that girl."

The more she thought about Ernest and Kate the more confused grew poor Miss Theodora. She trained up some wandering tendrils of morning-glory, and with relief heard Diantha saying, respectfully:

"Mr. Somerset's in the house, ma'am. He's been waiting some time."

She set her watering-pot down hastily on the ground beside her. Here was some one whose advice she could safely ask. She had not seen Richard Somerset since Ernest went away in June,— not, indeed, since he had made the important announcement.

"I think myself," said her cousin, after they had talked for some time about Ernest's professional prospects, and had begun to touch on the other matter, "I think myself that you make a mistake in not calling on the girl—no matter how the affair turns out.   It would please Ernest, and it couldn't do much harm. I've come to think that the more you fall in with a young man's ideas at such a time, the more likely he is to come around in the end to your way of thinking.   For all Ernest is so gentle, he's pretty determined—just like John. You know he never could be made to give up a thing when once he'd set his mind on it."

"Yes, I know," responded Miss Theodora mildly.

"Well,'' continued her cousin, "I'm not sure but that you are making a mistake in this case. Now, really, I don't believe that the girl or her people are half bad. It's surprising occasionally to find some of these people one don't

know not so very different from those
we have been brought up with. I remember when I was on one of those
committees for saving the Old South, a
man on the committee who lived up
there at the South End invited us to
meet at his house. Now, he gave us a
supper that couldn't have been surpassed anywhere. The silver and china
were of the best, and everything in the
house was in perfectly good form,—fine
library, good pictures, and all,—and
positively the most of us had never
heard of the fellow until we met him on
that committee. Well, I dare say it's a
good deal the same way with this
Kurtz."

Almost unconsciously Miss Theodora
raised her hand in deprecation.

"Yes," he went on, "naturally you
don't want to think about it at present;
but he's made a lot of money, and the
East India trade that set up some of our
grandfathers wasn't so very different

from his business. Besides, Mr. Kurtz has some standing. I see he's treasurer for the Home for Elderly and Indigent Invalids,—and that means something. Think it over, Theodora, and don't let any girl come between you and Ernest."

Much more to the same purpose said Richard Somerset, thereby astonishing his cousin. To her he had always seemed conservatism embodied. But he had not lived in the midst of a rapidly growing city without feeling the pulse of the time. While his own life was not likely to be affected by the new ideas which he had begun to absorb, he was not afraid to give occasional expression to them. Richard Somerset was several years older than Miss Theodora. In early life he had had the prospect of inheriting great wealth. With no desire for a profession, he let his taste turn in the direction of literary work. He had large intentions, which he was in no haste to carry out. With letters to several eminent men in England, France and Germany, he, as soon as he was graduated, started on a European tour. He studied in a desultory way at one or two great universities, enjoyed foreign social life of the quiet and professional kind, and acquired colloquial ease in two or three modern languages. Then his tour, which had lasted nearly three years, was cut short by his father's death. For several years afterward, with large business interests to look after, he had scant time for literary work. He managed, however, to bring out one historical monograph—a study of certain phases of Puritan life in the Massachusetts Bay Colony. Thereafter, no other book came from his pen, though he contributed occasional brief articles to a well-known historical magazine, and over the signature of "Idem" sent many communications of local interest to a certain evening paper of exclusive circulation.

Finally Richard Somerset found himself so immersed in business that he
ceased even to aspire to literary renown.
But he continued to read voraciously,
and at length, when the great fire swept
away the two large buildings which he
and his sister owned, he was less disturbed than he ought to have been.

His sister, however, took this loss to
heart. She had married when not very
young a man with no money, and had
found herself not so very long after-
wards a widow with two daughters to
educate according to the station—as she
said—in which Providence had placed
them.

To make up, to an extent at least, for
her loss, her brother surrendered a good
share of the income remaining to him.
He did this with a secret satisfaction not
entirely due to the fact that he was helping his sister. He felt that he was paying a kind of premium for the freedom
from care which the burning up of his

property had brought him. He paid the premium cheerfully, betook himself to a sunny room in a house not far from the Athenaeum, and thereafter devoted himself to his books. His day was regularly divided; a certain amount of time to eating, sleeping, exercise, and to society, including the Club, for he was no hater of his fellow men and women—and a certain amount of time to the Athenaeum. At first he had intended to resume his historical research. But the periodical room of the Athenaeum at length claimed the most of his time. He read English newspapers, French reviews and American magazines, and this in itself was an occupation. Yet sometimes as he sat near one of the windowed alcoves, and looked out over the old graveyard, his conscience smote him.

When he saw the sunshine filtering through the overhanging boughs of the old trees upon the gray gravestones, his thoughts were often carried back to that historic past, in which he had once had so much interest. Then, as he glanced past the pyramidal Franklin monument, noting the busy rush of life in the great thoroughfare on the other side of the high iron fence, he would ponder a little over the contrasts between the Boston of today and the Boston of the past. His reflections if put on paper would have been valuable.

As it was, he did no more than give occasional expression to his views when among his intimate friends. He realized, nevertheless, that from them he received but scant sympathy. Like most persons with original ideas, he was thought to be just a little peculiar.

"Queer, you know; never sees things just as we do; but still awfully sensible," some of the club men would say, without observing the contradiction implied in this speech.

Yet in spite of an occasional criticism of this kind Richard Somerset was admittedly a popular man, constantly consulted in matters where real judgment was the chief requisite. In emergencies, when special committees were formed to attend to things philanthropic or literary, he was always the first man thought of as a suitable member.

Miss Theodora often wondered what she should have done without him; but reflecting long over this his latest advice about her attitude toward Eugenie, she felt not wholly satisfied.

XXIII.

Ben was again in Boston. A position on the staff of a great railroad had been offered him, and Boston for some time would be his headquarters. He was not sorry to be at home. His mother and father seemed to him to be growing less capable. His sisters needed him, and his salary was large enough to enable him to do for them the many little things that add so much to young girls' pleasure.

To Miss Theodora his return was almost as great a boon as to his own family. At least once a day he called to see what he could do for her, and usually he went within the house to have a little chat with her. It was not strange that they talked chiefly of Ernest. Ben's nature was strongly sympathetic, and he knew what subject lay nearest Miss Theodora's heart. Yet he disturbed her by telling her plainly that he really thought that she ought to take some notice of Eugenie.

"But they're not engaged," apologized Miss Theodora, who discerned in Ben a feeling that she was unjust to Ernest.

"I know they're not," he replied; "but it's much the same thing as if they were. Ernest won't change, and her father will soon give his consent."

Yet Miss Theodora could not get herself into a relenting mood, though Ben, like Richard Somerset, added to her confusion.

Sometimes when Ben called at Miss Theodora's he found Kate there.   In her presence little was said about Ernest, and nothing about Eugenie.

He had thought himself almost disloyal to Kate when he had asked Miss Theodora to recognize Eugenie.   His only defence was his friendship for Ernest, and he was pleased enough that Ernest had never sought his advice in this love affair of his.   How could he have counselled Ernest to be more appreciative of Kate without disclosing his view of her feelings, and how could he have encouraged Ernest in his love for Eugenie without being disloyal to Kate?

But what was Ernest made of, he queried, to pass Kate by for a girl like Eugenie, well enough in her way, perhaps, but oh! so different from Kate? Then, as he glanced at the latter, he could but wonder if certain changes which he noticed in her—a quietness of expression, an unwonted slowness of response, so unlike her former habit of repartee—were induced by regret at this new turn in Ernest's affairs. It was a matter about which he himself could say nothing. His own feeling for her was now too strong. He wondered if any one would even suspect how much he had cared for Kate. Kate of course must never know. He would not run the risk of destroying their friendship by rash expressions of a regard warmer than she had dreamed of. Surely he was not presumptuous in believing that Kate valued this friendship. Certainly there was no one else to whom he could open his own heart as freely as to her; and he flattered himself that she confided not a little in him. This autumn she had come to town in advance of her

mother, and was spending a month with
Miss Theodora.   He saw her often,
therefore, sometimes when he called at
Miss Theodora's, sometimes in one of
the neighboring side streets, on her way,
as he usually thought, to visit some of
her colored beneficiaries.

Ben knew that Kate, since she had
come of age, had spent no small share of
her income in furthering schemes for the
improvement of various poor people.
Some of these schemes he fully approved; others seemed to him of doubtful value.   Yet his disapproval, though
he might not have admitted it to himself,
was based on no firmer ground than his
wish that Kate, as far as possible, should
be spared the sight and knowledge of
disagreeable things.

Meeting her one day, "It seems to me
that you are always running away from
Miss Theodora's," he had said in a tone
of mock reproof.

"Oh, well, only when I go to my

cooking class. You see, it's such fascinating work, and the new teacher doesn't get on with those children half as well as I do. She's a good teacher, but it's the human nature, the black human nature, that she does not exactly understand. When things are running smoothly I don't expect to see her more than once or twice a week."

"Once or twice a week," echoed Ben, about twice as often as you ought to inhale the odors of Phillips Street."

"Oh, nonsense, you should see our room, as clean and bright as fresh paint and paper can make it, with its perfectly ideal arrangements in the shape of stove and dishes."

Ben smiled, though not exactly in approval. Yet more and more he realized her power in the neighborhood.

"See that new machine," said Miss Chatterwits, when he called on her one day, and she pointed proudly to a new combination of polished wood and shining metal. "Well, Kate bought me that. She gives me a good deal of fine sewing to do, and thought this machine would be handier than my old one, which I'd had—well, I won't say how long, but almost ever since they were first made.. It had grown kind of rickety, and hadn't any modern improvements."

"This one looks as if it could do almost everything," said Ben, glancing at it a second time.

"Well, I do get a sight of comfort with it. Kate, or p'r'aps I ought to say Miss Digby, allows me so much a week, and expects to have all my time. She has me do white stitching for her,— which I always do by hand,—and make garments of various kinds for her poor people, which I do on the machine." Miss Chatterwits said "poor people" in a very dignified tone. She was never quite sure that she enjoyed sewing for these dependents.

"You must be kept pretty busy, then," responded Ben.

"Well, not so busy as I might be," she answered. "Some weeks there's very little for me to do. But I get my money just the same," she added quickly. "To tell you the truth, I guess Kate wanted to keep me out of the Old Ladies' Home, where I certainly should be living this very minute if she hadn't planned things out for me. Of course you wouldn't mention this to any one else ;"—and she looked at Ben earnestly, for she suddenly remembered that the outside world did not know of this little arrangement.

"Of course I won't mention it," said the young man ; "but it's just like Kate, isn't it?"

"Yes, it is ; you see, she found out just how I was situated after my sisters died. There wasn't a cent of our savings left, and people began to get so dressy that they thought they had to have their things made out of the house, or employ young women.   Not that I couldn't have done as well as anybody, with the help of paper patterns, but people didn't think so, and I was at my wits' end. What to do I didn't know —"

"There was Miss Theodora," began Ben.

"Yes, she was ready enough, and she kept me along with the little work she had.   But Kate herself kind of interfered with that.   She said Miss Theodora had worn old clothes long enough, and she some way persuaded her to get that dress for Ernest's graduating exercises made down town.   Well, it seems a pity, when Miss Theodora's got almost a whole trunk of things to be cut over, that she shouldn't use them up. However, just when I was at my wits' end, Kate came along, and says she: 'How much ought you to earn every week to live comfortably? I'll add a third to that if you'll save all your time

for me; I see that I'll have to have lots
of sewing done the next year or two;'—
and though I knew it was me she was
thinking of more than herself, I was
glad enough to say 'yes' to her offer."

After this Miss Chatterwits wondered
how she had happened to open her heart
so to Ben. A third person would have
accounted for it by the fact that Ben and
Miss Chatterwits were both deeply interested in the same object.

XXIV.

Henceforth, after his conversation with Miss Chatterwits, Ben was more attentive to her than he had ever been before. When he met her he always accompanied her to the door, and if she had been at the grocer's or the baker's, he insisted on carrying her parcels.

"I used to think it was very shiftless to buy bakers' bread," she said one day, apologizing for the large loaf which Ben had transferred under his own arm. "But it ain't shiftless when you're only one. It wouldn't pay me to have a regular baking. The bread would get stale before I could eat it all,"—to which Ben assented.

"Ben always was a good boy," she confided to a neighbor, "which it isn't to be wondered at when you remember who his great-grandfather was. It isn't every young man, especially with as good a position as he's got, would walk up the street with an old woman like me." She appreciated his kindness the more because the rising generation of the neighborhood paid very little attention to her. They beheld only a little old woman, somewhat bent in the back, with sparse, gray curls, queer clothes, and an affected walk, instead of the dignified person, as she pictured herself to be, whose acquaintance with better days gave her an elegance of aspect which the boys ought at least to respect.

Ben, therefore, realizing that the little woman was always glad to see him, made her frequent, if brief, calls. Sometimes he carried her a book, or some fruit, or at least a breath of news from the outside world—which she liked to hear about, even while professing to despise it.   Perhaps Ben was not altogether single-minded in this matter— who of us is absolutely single-minded about anything?   Perhaps he visited Miss Chatterwits as much to hear her talk about Kate as to give pleasure to the old lady herself.

Perhaps Miss Chatterwits, reading his mind better than he did himself, often talked purposely of the subject that lay so very near his heart.   It was certainly no accident when she turned nervously to Ben one day with the words:

"There's something I feel's if I ought to tell you;"—and the young man rose from the little wooden rocker in which he had vainly tried to look comfortable, saying cheerfully:

"Is there?   Well, do tell me."

Then Miss Chatterwits bridled a little, and blushed, and said: "Well, of course, there's some people that think an old maid hasn't any real knowledge of matters relating to the affections"—she did not exactly like to come out broadly with "love affairs"—"but, so far as I'm concerned myself, I know pretty well what's going on around me and how people feel about most things—though I don't always tell what I know."

Then Ben felt himself growing a little uncomfortable, while the blood rushed to his face. It was leap year, but surely Miss Chatterwits was not going to wax sentimental toward him. She did not leave him long in doubt.

"As I tell Kate," she continued, "people don't always know the exact state of their own feelings. She thinks she'll be an old maid, but she's making a mistake if she thinks she'd be happier,—not that I haven't got along well enough myself. But Kate isn't calculated to live alone.

Someway she and her mother ain't very congenial, and I guess Ralph's rather domineering. I know he's tried to stop some of her cooking classes—and—"

Here Miss Chatterwits stopped—and then began to talk again.

"Ben, you know that photograph that you and Ernest had taken in a group— Ernest on his bicycle, and you standing alongside?"

"Oh, a little tintype."

"Yes, so it was. I guess it's six or seven years since it was taken."

"Yes, it must be."

"Well, one day I'd been fitting on something for Kate, and she left her watch behind. There was a little locket hanging to the end of it, and I went to pick the watch up; it caught on the handle of a drawer, and as I pulled it it accidentally jerked open, and there, inside that locket, was that picture."

"Oh, my dear Miss Chatterwits, it was too large to go inside any locket."

"Oh, I don't mean the whole picture, but the head—your head—it had been cut clear off. There was your head in Kate's locket."

Ben looked annoyed. He felt that something had been told him which he had no right to hear. He did not know what to say.

"I'm losing my own head," he murmured; but to Miss Chatterwits—putting on a bold face—he said: "Oh, you must have seen Ernest's picture; you know we look alike;"—and he laughed, for no two faces could be more unlike.

But Miss Chatterwits shook her head. "Oh, no; I'm not blind. There's many other things I could tell you, too; but I speak for your own good, for I'm most as fond of you as I am of Kate."

With these mysterious words, she opened the door for Ben, who seemed in haste to go, to ponder perhaps what she had said, or to put it out of his mind,— which, Miss Chatterwits wondered as he left her.

In suggesting to Ben what she believed to be Kate's feeling toward him, Miss Chatterwits was governed by various motives. Chief, probably, was her belief that her interference was really for Kate's good. "I wish that somebody had ever interfered for me," she said to herself, thinking of the one young man who had ever interested her, who she really believed had been prevented only by bashfulness from reciprocating her feelings. "I believe it's the duty of older people to try to bring things about," she thought. "At any rate, I don't believe Kate could be offended at what I said. I know when people are just fitted for each other. Miss Theodora don't understand about those things. She's all wrong about it's being Ernest and Kate. She isn't observing. Mrs. Stuart Digby would a sight rather it had been Ernest than Ben, little as she cared for Ernest; and I'd be glad enough to help on things, just for the sake of bothering Mrs. Digby. She never looks my way when she meets me, and I did hear that she told Kate she wished she wouldn't come to see me so much. Well, it's easier to look behind you than ahead, and I'll not say another word to Ben or Kate, but I'll wait and see."

Ben tried to attach no importance to what Miss Chatterwits had said.

"Suppose Kate does wear my picture in her locket—we're very old friends, and that does not signify anything."

The next day he chanced to meet Kate at the crowded Winter Street crossing, after she had been shopping. Even as he piloted her across the street, threading his way under the very feet of the car and carriage horses, his eye fell on the old-fashioned locket dangling from her fob.

"Whose picture have you in that locket? Whose picture have you in that locket?" echoed itself in a danger-ous refrain in his mind, until he feared that he should utter the words aloud.

It was a clear, crisp afternoon; the few autumn leaves that had fallen cracked under their feet; the afternoon sun shone on the State House dome until it looked itself like a second sun.

"Did you ever know so delightful a day?" said Kate.

"Never," said Ben positively. They took the longest way home, skirting the edge of the Frog Pond; and then—what would Mrs. Digby have said?—they sat down on a settee.

Except for some small boys on the opposite shore sailing a refractory toy boat, they were almost alone, though in the very heart of the city. Kate gazed abstractedly at the clear reflection of the tall trees in the mirror before them. She dared not look at Ben, for she felt his eyes upon her, and this knowledge made her heart beat uncomfortably.

She fingered nervously the little package that she had brought from down town, and tried to think of something to say to break the spell. Ben saw that she avoided his eyes, and after waiting vainly for a glance from her, he could bear the strain no longer. Speak he must, and would. For what reason could Kate have for treasuring that memento of himself, if it were not that?—

"Kate," he cried, leaning toward her, while the refrain in his brain found vent at last in words, "whose picture have you in that locket?"

Kate started violently, grasping the locket, as if detected in some crime.

"Why do you ask?" she said, facing him resolutely, her cheeks crimson, her eyes bright. But her voice trembled, and Ben, with a lover's perception, taking courage from these signs, laid his hand gently on hers and drew the tell-tale locket from her unresisting grasp.

"Shall I open it, Kate?" he said slowly. "Remember, it will be my answer."

She looked into his eyes at last, and—well—what the answer was he read there you or I need not inquire. It is enough to know that half an hour later Ben and Kate walked homeward, apparently unconscious of everything but each other's existence. They even passed by one or two acquaitances without bowing, although without great effort they really could have seen them perfectly well.

When they reached Miss Theodora's door they stood for a minute looking down the hill.

"How blue the water is!" said Kate, gazing at the river, "and what an exquisite tint in the sky! Did you ever see anything so lovely?"

"Yes, I see something far lovelier now," said Ben, regarding Kate herself intently. Her face seemed to reflect the ruddy tint she admired.

"I meant the sunset," she said firmly.

"I should call it sunrise," smiled Ben, —and thus they entered the house.

XXV.

Poor Miss Theodora! She could never have imagined herself so indifferent to anything that concerned Kate as she was at first to the news of her engagement. But at length, after she had several times seen Kate and Ben together, she wondered that she had not long before realized their fitness for each other. Perhaps, after all, she had made a mistake in believing that Kate and Ernest could have been happy together. Certainly, she had been very blind in her estimate of Kate's feelings.

She never knew, for pride forbade the young girl to dwell on the rather painful subject, how difficult it was for Kate and Ben to gain Mrs. Digby's consent to their engagement. It could hardly be said, indeed, that she gave her consent. She simply submitted to the inevitable. Kate was of age, and had her own money, an independence, if not a fortune; and Mrs. Digby, after using every argument, decided to make the best of what she could not help. Ralph, at least, would commit no social folly like this of his sister's—Ralph, that model of discretion and mirror of good form. She did not even, as Miss Theodora had dreaded, reprove her cousin for allowing this love affair to develop unchecked by her. Whatever she may have thought of Miss Theodora's blindness, she decided to make Kate's engagement a family affair—an affair of her own small family, in which, apparently, she intended not to include her cousin.

Then Miss Theodora, feeling her heart soften as she watched Kate and Ben, wondered if she had not been too hard with Ernest. Ought she not to show some interest in Eugenie? Though this query never shaped itself in words spoken to Kate or any one else, it pressed itself upon her constantly. A sentence from Ernest's last letter haunted her: "I cannot be perfectly happy until I know that you and Eugenie have met. She has not written to me for some time, and I am almost sure this is because she is so much hurt at the coldness of my relatives. I did expect something different from you and Kate."

This letter touched Miss Theodora more than a little; but Kate made no response when her cousin read it to her. Though she could not tell exactly why, Kate's silence annoyed her. She even began to wonder what she should wear when she made the first call, and she recalled all Ernest had said about Eugenie's critical taste in dress. She was glad that Kate had insisted on her having an autumn street gown made at a fairly fashionable dressmaker's.

Miss Chatterwits happened to be sewing at Miss Theodora's on the day when the latter made her decision about Eugenie.

In spite of the new dressmaker, Miss Theodora still had some work for the old seamstress. Her method of working always afforded Kate great amusement.

For, as she talked, the points of a dozen pins projected from between her teeth, where she held them for convenience. She still wore close to her side the self-same little brown velvet cushion, or it looked like the same one, which had always astonished Ernest by its capacity. Though it was hardly an inch thick, Miss Chatterwits had a habit of running into its smooth surface long darning needles and shawl pins, as well

as fine needles and pins.   What became
of them was always a matter of deep
conjecture to Ernest, for they were
sometimes embedded until neither head
nor eyes could be seen.   It seemed as if
they must have pierced Miss Chatterwits' bony waist.   Could she possibly be
so thin as not to have any flesh to feel
the pricks?   Bones, of course, have no
feeling, used to think Ernest, watching
with a kind of fascination each motion
of Miss Chatterwits' hand, as she thrust
half a dozen long pins into the unresisting cushion.

On this important day when Miss
Theodora began to feel a change of
heart toward Eugenie, she sat down to
help Miss Chatterwits with her work.

"There's a morning paper," said the
seamstress.   "Tom Fetchum handed it
to me on his way down town; said he
had read it all but the deaths and mar-
riages, which he knew I'd like to see.   I
ain't had time to look at it yet, so you

might read them to me, Miss Theodora."

Miss Theodora, putting on her glasses, turned to the appointed place.

"Not a soul I know among those deaths! I'm disappointed," said Miss Chatterwits, after Miss Theodora had read the list. "Why, what is it?" she added; for Ernest's aunt was looking up with a curiously dazed expression, as she handed the paper to Miss Chatterwits, and pointed to a brief notice:

"KURTZ—DIGBY.—At Troy, N. Y., on the 24th inst., by Rev. John Brown, Eugenie, daughter of Simon Kurtz of Boston, to Ralph, son of the late Stuart Digby of the same city."

"Well, I never!" said Miss Chatterwits. "An elopement, I do believe! I'm glad I'm most through this skirt, so's I can run over to Mrs. Fetchum's and tell her. I guess she didn't read the paper very carefully this morning. If she'd seen it she'd 'a' been over here to find out how we took it. It's always safe to read the papers.

"Well, how do you feel, Miss Theodora?" she asked at last.

But Miss Theodora never told any one exactly how she felt when she heard of the strange ending of Ernest's love affair. To Ernest, of course, she gave a full measure of sympathy; and she was almost sorry that, as things had turned out, he would never know that she had made up her mind to make Eugenie's acquaintance. Since she had, though for only a brief time, almost changed her point of view, she felt herself to be hypocritical in receiving his praise for her acumen: "You knew better than I what she was like."

Kate was indignant at her brother's treachery.

"I shall never forgive him for deceiving Ernest so. But I can't say that I'm surprised. I knew that she and Ralph had had a great flirtation even before she met Ernest. It was that which made me so unwilling to call on her. But I never thought that Ralph would marry her. Mamma, I believe, is going to receive her as if everything had been perfectly above board. But I know it's only pride that leads her to take this stand. She really feels the whole thing very keenly."

Ben, when he heard of the elopement, could not help recalling the episode of the stolen skates, and he wondered if Ralph had made love to Eugenie from the mischievous motives by which he had so often in their boyhood allowed himself to be influenced against Ernest. If so, he was likely to be the meter out of his own punishment. For a bride stolen merely to annoy another person is likely to make more trouble than any other stolen possession.

Strangely enough, Ernest himself recovered most quickly from the mortification of the whole affair. There was

at first the shock to his pride, mingled
with contempt for the deceit practised
on him by Ralph and Eugenie. But he
was so young as to recover quickly, and
the element of contempt helped him to
brush the whole matter aside.

You, perhaps, may think less well of
Ernest for finding consolation so readily, but you must remember that he
never was a sentimentalist. Moreover,
neither you nor I may know exactly
what the workings of his mind may have
been. Doubtless there was many a
sleepless night, and many a bitter tear,
before he was ready to show a stern
front to the world. In Boston it might
have been a much harder thing for him
to bear the blow which fate had leveled
at him. After all, Massachusetts and
Colorado are far apart; and if propin-
quity is fate bearing, distance and separation are more destructive of sentimental
illusions than the average sentimentalist
admits. In Ernest's case, hard work

was absorbing, and even Grace Easton, William Easton's pretty young daughter, was a long time in winning the place which she afterward held in his heart.

XXVI.

You who look at the simple events which I have been relating (from the outside and at a distance) may have other criticisms to make of Ernest. You may think it impossible that a youth so well placed, as he was at Harvard, should have turned his back upon its paths of pleasantness for the narrower way that meant so much hard work. Yet Ernest had not allowed himself to be led or governed by an illusion. In the whole world the serious student, the man who has his own way to make, can find no better opportunity than at Harvard. No one could realize this better than Ernest himself, in that time of storm and stress when he had felt that the chart of his life must be mapped out by his own hand. But his, he saw, was a special case, and the surest way to free himself from all entanglements and to place himself at the command of duty, was, he thought, to start out on an entirely new course. It was his Puritan inheritance, this devotion to duty when once duty had shown clearly her kindly but resolute visage.

Yet my story has been ill told if it has seemed to be more the story of Ernest than of Miss Theodora. For very few of us does life hold any marked surprises, any startling events. A whole life is often merely the summary of many very commonplace happenings. Its real events are more likely to be those moral crises when the soul must put itself in harmony with all those external happenings which it has no power to control. Nor is it one of the least of life's lessons that it would be indeed a fatal gift, if it were ours — this longed for power to turn the tide of events.

Take, for example, the case of Miss Theodora; what a feeble figure she had been in her efforts to turn the current of affairs that made up her life. How helpless her will to accomplish her desires!

If John had not married Dorothy—if Ernest had been willing to take his grandfather's profession — if he had never met Eugenie—if he and Kate had never cared for each other, — with all these "ifs" turned into verities, how different, Miss Theodora thought, had been her outlook on life. But we, who regard these things from the point of view of the impartial onlooker, know that the fulfilling of her desires would not have made her happiness, nor for the happiness of her nephew.

If in trying to show you this I have seemed to dwell too long on the ordinary happenings in a simple life, remem-

ber that these, after all, were not the
things which I count of chief importance.

To me the great events in Miss Theodora's life were those three occasions
when she had to summon her strength
to great decisions. These soul crises
counted for more than any other happenings in her life. First, there was that
struggle when she had to choose between her lover and her nephew; then,
almost as severe, though different in
kind, the battle in which at last she had
given in to Ernest in his choice of a profession; and last, although it had had
no outward result, her merging of her
own prejudice against Eugenie in a
readiness to do what would probably
make Ernest happier.

Hardly less bitter than these three
struggles was the one which Miss Theodora waged to decide whether or not it
was her duty to join Ernest in the West.
At last she yielded in this more quickly

though with greater pain than in the two cases when she had given in to Ernest about Harvard and about Eugenie.

She left Boston with the less reluctance, perhaps, because of certain changes — some persons called them "improvements"—that had begun to appear in her well-loved West End. The tall apartment houses which had begun to creep in even before she left the city, the electric cars now dashing through Charles street, were innovations that cut her to the heart.

The breaking up of her modest little home soon followed.

"You will spend half of every year with us," said Kate, now pleasantly situated in a house whose western windows overlooked the river. She had already begun to make life pleasant for Ben's sisters, one of whom was always staying with her.

"That will depend upon Ernest," Miss Theodora had answered, smiling. As a matter of fact, she did not return to Boston, even for a visit, until after Ernest's marriage; and so with her removal to Colorado, her story — as a West End story—may be said to end.

But if I should tell you more about Miss Theodora, I would describe the delightful New England home which, with Diantha's help, she made for Ernest in Denver. Nor would I be able to omit telling of the romance which came into her own life.

At first she tried to avoid meeting William Easton, now a widower; but efforts of this kind, of course, were useless. They met calmly enough; and as they talked together, the years that had passed seemed as nothing.

"So you have come West, after all, Theodora—and for Ernest's sake, too, though it was for his sake you refused to come so long ago."

"Yes," she said, "for Ernest's sake it seems, though when I see how much he owes to you, I realize that you are more than kind—almost cruelly kind—"

Then William Easton, smiling somewhat sadly, said nothing in reply, though indeed there was no need of words. We all know how a story of this kind ends in books; and even in real life old lovers sometimes renew the pledges of youth.

(The End.)

www.ingramcontent.com/pod-product-compliance
Lightning Source LLC
Chambersburg PA
CBHW030757020726
47499CB00006B/1667